saving billie

PETER CORRIS is known as the 'godfather' of Australian crime fiction through his Cliff Hardy detective stories. He has written in many other areas, including a co-authored autobiography of the late Professor Fred Hollows, a history of boxing in Australia, spy novels, historical novels and a collection of short stories revolving around the game of golf. He is married to writer Jean Bedford and lives on the Illawarra coast, south of Sydney. They have three daughters.

PETER CORRIS

saving billie

A CLIFF HARDY NOVEL

Thanks to Jean Bedford, Trish Donaldson and Jo Jarrah

The suburb of Liston does not exist, nor, as far as I am aware, do the Island Brotherhood or the Children of Christ. Any resemblance to an actual place or organisations is coincidental.

First published in 2005

Allen & Unwin
83 Alexander Street
Crows Nest NSW 2065
Australia
Phone: (61 2) 8425 0100
Fax: (61 2) 9906 2218
Email: info@allenandunwin.com
Web: www.allenandunwin.com

National Library of Australia
Cataloguing-in-Publication entry:

Corris, Peter, 1942– .
Saving Billie: a Cliff Hardy novel.

ISBN 1 74114 652 6.

1. Hardy, Cliff (Fictitious character) – Fiction.
2. Private investigators – New South Wales – Sydney – Fiction. I. Title.

A823.3

Set in 12/14 pt Adobe Garamond by Midland Typesetters
Printed in Australia by McPherson's Printing Group

10 9 8 7 6 5 4 3 2 1

For Bradon and Trish

part one

1

It wasn't my kind of work, but I was doing a favour for a friend. Hank Bachelor, who'd given me some help in recent times, had got his Private Enquiry Agent licence and was scratching a living at whatever he could pick up.

'It's a sort of security job, Cliff,' he said on the phone. 'At a party.'

'Bouncer,' I said.

'No, no, this is a high-class affair. Top people; charity function. Politicians, media types, the glitterati.'

'Shepherding drunks to the dunny. Calling them taxis. Seeing no one nicks the silverware.'

'Yeah, maybe a bit of that. Come on, Cliff. I'm sick as I can be with this virus and I need to stay in tight with the firm that hired me. With you as a substitute, licensed and all, I won't lose any brownie points.'

Hank is an American who has embraced Australia in every way but still uses American idioms. I agreed to stand in for him at the Jonas Clement charity evening in Manly out of friendship, and curiosity about Clement.

'You'll have to wear a soup 'n fish,' Hank said.

I groaned. 'I hate those penguin suits. They make me feel like . . . a penguin.'

'Women like 'em. There'll be some babes at this shindig, believe me. You might get lucky.'

So I hired the gear from a place on Parramatta Road opposite one of the university colleges and not far from my house in Glebe. I walked there, getting as much exercise as I can these days to keep the flab at bay. I'd been there before.

'Still a forty-two long, ninety-three round the tummy, Mr Hardy?' the outfitter said.

'I think so.'

Stick-thin himself, he ran the tape over me. 'Best to check, some of our clients do tend to expand. Hmm, ninety-four centimetre waist. Not bad for your height and . . .'

'Don't say it. You're only as old as you want to be.'

'Interesting philosophy. Single or double-breasted? Two piece or three? Cummerbund or not?'

'Make a wild guess.'

Wearing the suit, with the studs and the dopey bow tie, I presented at Jonas Clement's Manly mansion at the appointed time and showed the hiring firm's credentials with my name substituted for Hank's and my PEA ticket. A man with a solid build and an aggressive manner looked me over as if he'd like to drop his shoulder and bullock me down the sandstone steps. Clement's house was on the water and hard to get to—a matter of parking where you could, tracking down a brightly lit laneway and going through a gate, where one set of steps led up to the house and another led down to a garden and recreational area near the water.

'Not sure about this,' he said, examining the pass.

'I'm filling in for this other bloke. With him you get youth and polish, with me you get experience. Maybe Mr Clement could decide.'

He handed the pass and licence back and gestured for me to go down the steps. 'Mr Clement has got better things to do. You go down and keep an eye on things. Circulate but don't annoy anyone. Watch out for—'

'Drunks and light fingers. I've done this sort of thing before.'

'Don't get pissed yourself.'

'What's your name? Just so I know who to come to if there's any trouble.'

'Rhys Thomas, one of Mr Clement's assistants.'

'Any relation to Dylan?'

'Distantly, and not proud of it, smartarse.'

One to him. I went down the steps and paused where they turned. The view out over the water was the kind that put another half million on the value of a property. They tell us the harbour's full of heavy metal, strontium 90 and whatever, and I suppose it is. Doesn't stop it looking like perfection on a clear night with the lights shining on it.

I tore myself away from Sydney at its best and reached the bottom of the steps where a marquee had been set up over a lawn the size of a bowling green. A portable dance floor was waiting to be shuffled on but the bar was already doing light business although it was early and there couldn't have been more than twenty people around. Two barmen were doling out the drinks and a couple of waiters were circulating with trays.

Three max, Cliff, I said to myself and plucked a glass of white wine from a tray.

Hank had told me that about a hundred guests were expected and from the look of the ice buckets full of bottles and the portable fridges and the bottles of spirits lined up, they weren't going to be thirsty. Away to the left a trestle table about four metres long was laden with food and three young women in cocktail dresses were standing ready to ladle out the potato salad and smoked salmon. A few of the early twenty were eyeing the tucker but no one wanted to be first hog to the trough. I nodded politely to a few people and tried to look as if I belonged.

I sipped the wine. A dry white—that's about as close to identifying a wine as I can get. Crisp, a pundit might have said. I moved out from under the canvas and looked up at the house. It rose from its manicured garden like a medieval fortress—sandstone rising three levels. A flagpole was just visible and an evening breeze was just strong enough to cause its flag to flutter, showing you quick flashes of stripes and stars.

'Don't worry,' a tall man who'd come out to join me said. 'There's an Aussie flag a bit further around.'

'That's good,' I said. 'Patriotism plus. Are you the host?'

'No way.' He was in immaculate evening clothes, drinking champagne. He glanced down at his empty glass and moved away.

Jonas Clement owned a city FM radio station and a couple of regional stations. He had a stud farm at Camden and substantial interests in a number of race-horses and a successful football club. What distinguished him from other merely rich men was that he did a stint as a shock-jock on his own station. His politics were far right and I'd been told his hero was American humorist PJ O'Rourke, whom he didn't equal in wit, although some said he gave it a good try. He was ardently pro-American and this evening's event was a money-raiser for American families who'd lost sons and daughters in Afghanistan and Iraq. The right would be out in force and I wasn't expecting to have too many stimulating conversations.

The crowd came in with a rush soon after 10 pm and the barmen and waiters and food servers got busy. A five-piece band started up the kind of white-bread music five-piece bands play and the noise level rose steadily.

I did a patrol of the house, at least the lower level. There was a kitchen that looked like a set for a TV cooking show, a tiled toilet with a urinal and four stalls, a pool and ping-pong room, a spa and sauna, and a room about the size of a squash court with hooks all around it for coats. There was a women's powder room. Pink.

Clement styled himself as a sportsman—probably why I kept thinking of his affluence in terms of sporting arenas. To add to the image there were sporting pictures on the walls here and there, but the impression I got was of someone trying too hard.

The party was in full swing by the time I got back to the marquee. Hank had said the punters were paying two thousand per head to be there and the joint was packed, so the take was probably good for a few prosthetic limbs and skin grafts. The men were all dressed as I was, except that some wore white jackets and they no doubt owned the clothes. The women were uniformly expensively turned out in dresses and trouser suits and other creations difficult to describe. They varied from comfortably upholstered matrons to rail-thin creatures who looked as though they lived on mineral water and celery sticks.

The combo was playing something reminiscent of Barry Manilow and the dancers were making the best of it. As so often happens at events like this, there were two outstanding dancers. The woman was a brunette in a red dress. She swirled about, showing an extreme length of very good leg. The man was built and moved like a gymnast and every step they made was in perfect synch. Most of the other dancers stopped to watch, and some of the women looked daggers at their men who were showing excessive interest in the legs.

The barmen and waiters were hard at it and a lot of the calories on the food table had been transferred to the guests. I took my second drink and Thomas, the man who'd quizzed me on my arrival, appeared at my shoulder.

'I told you not to drink.'

'You told me not to get drunk. I won't. You also said to circulate and look natural. That's what I'm doing.'

He smelled strongly of alcohol himself and something stronger than wine. 'Keep your eyes open. Mr Clement's going to make a speech soon. There could be demonstrators.'

'What, getting past you? Never.'

'You're pissing me off, Hardy, but for your information they came up from the water one time. Worked their way up from one of the other houses.'

'What was the occasion in aid of? Aboriginal land rights?'

I was sorry as soon as I said it. Hank needed this gig not to be a fuck-up and I wasn't helping. I turned towards

Thomas to say something conciliatory, but he'd gone. Failing an invasion from the water, it looked like being a quiet night. Fine by me.

There was a stirring among the guests that signalled a significant moment and Jonas Clement appeared almost magically on the bandstand as the musicians let out a quiet riff and fell silent. Clement looked to be in his late forties; he was tall and well built with a full head of dark hair greying at the sides. He had a tan and white teeth and he wore his evening clothes as if they were something to relax in. The woman standing beside him was tall and blonde and everything else she should be. She stayed slightly behind Clement, but he reached back and squeezed her hand before stepping up to the mike.

The tall champagne drinker who'd commented on the flags earlier spoke next to my ear: 'Ten to one, he clears his throat. Common touch. Unaccustomed as I am . . . like hell.'

Clement cleared his throat. 'Ladies and gentlemen, friends . . . it's so good to see you here tonight supporting this brave and worthy cause. My wife Patty and I are hoping to raise enough money to . . .'

I tuned out after he got on to the need for laws to punish what he called traitors here and overseas, and moved to where I couldn't hear him as clearly. Most of the crowd was paying rapt attention, but there were a few cynics intent on drinking, like the one who'd picked Clement's mannerism so accurately. A couple of the men and a few of the women were clearly drunk and having trouble standing, let alone listening. One guy was busily cracking lobster claws and couldn't have heard what was coming over the microphone anyway.

Hank's remark about there possibly being some available women at the bash came back to me and I looked the group over with that in mind, not optimistically. That's when I spotted her. She looked and moved differently from the other guests. Not that she wasn't dressed appropriately. She wore a dark blue dress with a black jacket and had the requisite jewellery. Dark hair, fashionably spiked. She was medium tall and athletically built, marking her out from the models and the well-fed wives. More than that, she was slowly moving through the crowd towards the bandstand and there was purpose in her movement. At a party, especially a well-fuelled one like this, people move differently than they do at work or in the street. She looked as if she was working. In that context it seemed threatening and I headed in her direction, pushing people aside.

Clement was winding up and I could hear him again.

'And so, thank you, each and every one, from the bottom of our hearts and I beg you to reach to the bottom of your pockets. Donation letters are on the way. Tell your secretary to expect one and put it at the top of your pile. Thank you, thank you.'

He finished. The dark-haired woman got there before me and grabbed the mike.

'Mr Clement, do you have any comment about your connection with American arms manufacturers who supplied weapons to rebels in Sierra Leone and—'

Rhys Thomas was there in a flash, but not before Clement hissed 'You slimy bitch' audibly. Thomas jerked the microphone from the woman's grasp and shouted to the musicians to start playing: they did, loudly. Thomas's grip on the woman's arm was vice-like and she was wincing with pain. I moved in quickly and dug into the nerve in his shoulder so that he let go. 'There's a guy filming this back there,' I hissed. 'Want to make it look worse?'

Clement, momentarily nonplussed, recovered quickly when he heard me. 'Let her go, Rhys. She's nothing. You,' he pointed at me, 'get her out of here.'

She was still gasping from the pain of Thomas's grip and let me escort her back past the musicians towards the steps leading to the house. By the time we'd gone up a step or two she'd recovered and resisted.

'What the fuck are you doing? There was no one filming.'

'I know, but he could've paralysed your arm. Let's see it.'

She slipped off her jacket and her bare, lightly tanned arm showed a redness that would probably become a deep, dark bruise where Thomas's meaty hand had been.

'Jesus,' she said. 'You're right.'

'Better get moving. Thomas'll be looking for the video maker. He'll be very pissed off when he doesn't find him.'

We went up a few steps and she gave a short laugh. 'No, not to worry. You can video with a mobile phone. He'll never know. Still, I made my point.'

'You did. Is it true?'

'You bet your life it's true.'

We'd reached the top of the steps with the gate in sight. She dug into her handbag and took out a tape recorder. 'I've got that prick on tape and also what I said to him. Good copy.'

'Journalist?'

'And author to be. Well, you'd better get back to work. You're a minder if ever I saw one.'

I was reluctant to let her go. She had an attractive intensity and a voice that made you want to listen to her. 'You could be wrong about that. I'm just filling in for someone.'

'You don't work for Clement?'

'I'd rather spend the rest of my life at a Kamahl concert.'

She laughed. 'That's a good line.'

'I stole it from somewhere.'

'I guessed that. Never mind.'

'I'm Cliff Hardy.'

She took a card from her bag and handed it to me, turned quickly and walked away. I had a weird feeling she was going to flutter her fingers at me without looking back, like Liza Minnelli in *Cabaret,* but she didn't.

2

'Thanks a lot, Cliff.' Hank's voice on the phone the next day was still full of wheeze and huskiness.

Since Hank, like many Americans, was incapable of irony, I had to accept that he meant it.

'I understand Clement thanked you,' he said.

'Not personally. He sort of conveyed his thanks. I think that's how he does things.'

'Anyway, I'm still on the books with those people so I owe you.'

I'd gone back to Clement's party and continued on with my uneventful duties. I got some black looks from Thomas but one of Clement's minions had told me the boss was happy with what I'd done. I had another drink on the strength of that and called it a night as the party was winding down around 1.30 am. I'd had my three drinks and managed a couple of sandwiches and chunks of cheese as blotter so I reckoned I was all right to drive home.

Back in my place at Glebe, I took off the dinner suit and went through the pockets. I'd shoved the card the woman had given me in with my keys and it was crumpled. I smoothed it out. It identified her as Louise Kramer, feature writer on the *Sydney News,* a paper I'd never heard of. It carried her work and mobile phone numbers, and her email address. I put the card aside and made a mental note to check on her with Harry Tickener, who knows everything worth knowing about journalism and journalists in Sydney. She'd shown a lot of courage fronting Clement like that and I liked her feistiness. I thought I might give her a call and ask how her arm was. She was on my mind as I went up to bed—thirty-five or thereabouts, no wedding ring, black Irish looking with the pale skin, dark hair and blue eyes. Why not?

As it turned out she paid me a visit in my Newtown office later that morning, making her one of the earliest clients in my new set-up. When the renovators moved in on St Peters Lane, Darlinghurst, where I'd had my office since I'd got my PEA licence, all us low rent types moved out. I worked from home for a while, didn't like it, and took over an office in Newtown at the St Peters end of King Street. St Peters cropping up again was a coincidence but I liked it and took it as a good omen. Gentrification hadn't reached there, at least as far as commercial space was concerned, and the office was one floor up at the front overlooking the street. The stairs were sound, if narrow, and not well lit, and the windows facing King Street were grimy. But who needed to watch cars and buses and trucks go by?

My office had room enough for a desk, a chair each for me and the client, a couple of filing cabinets and a bookcase. There was a small alcove off it where a coffee maker sat on top of a bar fridge, sharing a double adaptor. A phone-fax and computer and printer needed a power board to run from the single power point in the office. I'd been there for three quiet months. Parking was a problem. So far the government's terror alerts hadn't brought me any business.

There were two other offices on this level. One unoccupied and the other bearing a stencilled sign that read 'MIDNIGHT RECORDS'. So far I hadn't seen anyone go in or out, but maybe that figured. Toilet at the end of the hall with washbasin and tap. Pretty basic. Some clients like it, thinking that low overheads mean low fees; others take fright. Louise Kramer wouldn't have taken fright in Pamplona running the bulls. She plonked her backpack down on the floor and sat in the clients' chair. My coffee maker was emitting the croak it does when the brew is ready.

'Is that drinkable?' she said.

'Usually. Want some?'

I fixed her a mug with long-life milk and no sugar, like mine, and watched her try it. The spiked hair of last night was flattened down and she wore jeans and a V-necked, long-sleeved cotton top, sneakers. All business. The earrings and necklace had gone, of course, but her makeup was carefully applied and she was bright-eyed, close to hyper.

'That's good, thanks. I live on this stuff. You?'

I shrugged. 'Plus alcohol, adrenalin, carbohydrates.'

'I did some quick research on you, Mr Hardy, and I'm puzzled by your presence at that party.'

'I told you, I was filling in for a friend.'

'Mmm, I wonder if I believe that.'

'Look, Ms Kramer—' I waved the card I'd put on my desk to get the phone number—'I'm pleased to see you looking so up, but I'm puzzled by your presence here. How's the arm, by the way?'

She touched her upper arm. 'Bloody sore, but it would've been worse if you hadn't stepped in. That bastard Thomas grips like a bolt cutter.'

I drank some more coffee, not knowing how to play this. 'You talk as if you know him.'

'I know *of* him, like all Clement's functionaries. He was a steward at Randwick until he got sacked for doing things he shouldn't. He got the grip from controlling horses.'

'Interesting,' I said.

'Meaning, again, what am I doing here?'

'You're drinking my coffee with enjoyment apparently, and saying interesting things. I'm not busy, as you can see. I'm not grizzling.'

'Like I say, I've looked into you. For someone in your game you stack up pretty well. I'm thinking of hiring you.'

'Well, we'd both have to think about that. You'd have to believe me that I was a fill-in at that event and I'd have to know what you're on about.'

She nodded. 'I believe you.'

'That's a start.'

She drew in a deep breath. 'I'm writing a book about Clement. An exposé.'

'What's to expose?'

'A hell of a lot. Know how he got his kick-start capital?'

'No.'

'He puts it out that he got it speculating in stock in the dot com boom.'

'Sounds possible.'

'But he didn't. I've searched the records.'

I shrugged. 'They can run and they can hide.'

'Not from me. He got his start from some huge brokerage fees arranging loans. One was from the Niven-Jones bank, which was run by crooks, to Blue Rock Mining. As everyone knows, they went bust. There were a few others like that, but the really interesting one is from Tasman Investments to Peter Scriven. Twenty-five million, five million brokerage.'

That got my attention. I didn't follow the financial news but everyone able to watch TV had heard of Scriven. He'd been one of the media moguls of the nineties who'd slowly got in too deep and had skipped the country owing tens of millions and ruining many small businesses in the process. He'd left scores of employees high and dry and what he owed the tax office would put a dent in the current account deficit.

Louise Kramer enjoyed watching my reaction. 'I reckon he helped Scriven get away and got well paid for that, too.'

I finished my coffee. 'Hard to prove. Scriven's vanished.'

'There're others around who know things. If I could get some details from one person in particular, I could pull the plug on Clement.'

'Sounds personal.'

She drained her mug and put it on the desk where it made a ring to join all the other rings. 'No. Professional.'

'Was last night professional? Taking him on at his party? What did you have to gain?'

'When word got around that I was doing this book, Clement at first tried to buy me off. Offered me a job and all that. When that didn't work he threatened me and the publisher. Legal bullying. Followed by more direct personal stuff.'

'Like?'

'Slashed tyres. Heavy breathers. Creeps hanging around. I put my head down and got on with my research.

Just in case he might've thought I'd gone away, last night I was showing him I hadn't.'

'Well, it's very interesting, Ms Kramer, but—'

'Lou.'

'Okay, Lou, but I can't see how I can help. I use the finance pages to wrap the fat from the griller.'

'Ever hear of Eddie Flannery?'

'Of course. Private investigator, or was until he got delicensed.'

'Right. He worked for Clement as a bagman, fixer, minder. Got himself killed a few months back. Took a tumble down the McElhone steps at the Cross. I reckon Clement had it done because Flannery was blackmailing him.'

'Any proof?'

'I had it, sort of, but I lost it. I got on to Flannery's de facto wife, Billie Marchant. She told me she knew about some of the things Eddie had done for Clement and that she had proof Clement had Eddie killed. She was going to tell me more but she got scared and took off. That's where you come in, Mr Hardy.'

'Cliff.'

She nodded. 'I want you to find Billie Marchant so I can talk to her again. I *need* to know that inside stuff about Clement's business.'

I sat back and thought it over. I'd known Eddie slightly back in the days when there were more independent PEAs than now. Most work for corporations these days and spend their time on keyboards. Like me, Eddie was ex-army and one of the old school, from the time when surveillance was done personally rather than by programmed cameras, people carried cash that needed protecting, and car insurance scams were all the go. Unlike me, he was as crooked as they come, and after several warnings he lost his licence. I hadn't heard anything of him recently and didn't know that he was dead.

'If Clement's as ruthless as you say, he might've got to Billie as well.'

'I don't think so. When I talked to her she implied there was someone else inside Clement's organisation that had it in for him and was tipping her off. I think that person told her to lay low.'

'Any idea who that could be?'

'No. I'm working on it.'

'She could be anywhere—England, the US, South Africa, the Philippines . . .'

Lou dug in her bag and came up with a packet of Nicorettes. She released one and popped it in. 'I quit when I started on this book. Knew if I didn't, I'd smoke myself to death in the process.'

'Good move.'

She got the gum going. 'No, Billie wouldn't leave Sydney. Couldn't. Born and bred here and she's done everything low-life Sydney you can think of—stripped, whored, used and sold drugs, done time, informed—you name it. And I know something about her no one else much knows.'

'Which is?'

'Are you willing to take it on?'

'It's expensive, Lou, and there's no guarantee of success.'

'Look—' she leaned forward—'I know that. I got a decent advance for this book and I can afford to pay you. At least for a while.'

'What if you have to cough up to Billie?'

She knew she had me and she smiled. 'I'd negotiate with the publisher. C'mon, Cliff. Like you said, you haven't got anything much else going on. I don't hear feet on the stairs. The phone hasn't rung. I bet you haven't got a whole bunch of exciting emails to answer.'

I got a contract form out of a desk drawer and slid it across. 'I'm in.'

'Good. You'll be deductible, too.'

'How's that?'

'Everything a writer does is deductible. If you play golf and write about it, you can deduct your membership fees.'

'What if you play poker, bet on the horses and write about that. Can you deduct your losses?'

'That might be iffy. Where do I sign?'

I had her work and mobile phone numbers and email address on her card. I gave her my card with the same information and my address in Glebe. She gave me her street address and wrote me a cheque. I took notes on her investigation so far—Billie's last known address, her car registration, description when last seen and habits. Billie smoked as though the world was about to be hit by a tobacco famine, drank as if prohibition was coming back, and was known to take every mind-altering drug in the pharmacopoeia.

'Given that,' I said, 'she could be dead.'

'No way. Tough as an old boot. Forty if she's a day and, like I said, doesn't look anything like it with a bit of makeup and the light in the right place. And, to repeat myself now that you're really listening, there's something else I know about her that I suspect not many do and you should.'

'She bungy jumps?'

'I hope you're taking this seriously, Cliff.'

'My way of taking things seriously is not to take them too seriously until I have to.'

She thought that over, chewing hard, and nodded. 'Okay. Billie's got a child. A son.'

'Eddie's?'

'I doubt it. From what I hear and from photos, Eddie resembled a chook.'

That was true. Eddie was sharp-featured with a noticeably small head.

'This child—teenager by now, I guess—was on the way to being well built and good looking.'

'Billie's genes.'

'And black.'

Lou told me she'd got into a drinking session with Billie and that Billie had passed out. Lou snooped and found the photo—taped to the back of the middle drawer in a dresser—of the child standing beside Billie. The photo was faded and had been much handled. The boy appeared to be somewhere in the eight to ten age range and from Billie's clothes she guessed the picture to be a few years old.

'You pulled out all the dresser drawers?'

'Bugger you. This one was loose—it came free.'

'Have you got the photo?'

'No, it . . . it seemed so personal. I re-stuck it.'

'Background?'

She shrugged. 'Nothing identifiable to me.'

'Nothing scrawled on the back? Like, "Me and Jason, Bondi, 1998"?'

She looked at me as though she'd like to tear up the cheque. 'You don't believe me?'

'I'm wondering how you out-drank a hard doer the way you say Billie is.'

'Let me tell you something about myself, Mr Hardy. I've knocked around small time and country newspapers for twenty years. I'm thirty-eight with two failed marriages. I've survived cervical cancer and I've got a mortgage I struggle to pay. This is my shot and I'm giving it everything I've got. I out-drank Billie Marchant because I had to.'

'Okay. Sorry.'

'For your information, there was something on the back of the photo. It was scribble, but it looked like B and S.'

'Eddie's middle name was Stanley.'

'I didn't know that.'

'There you go. We're a team. Neither of us knows everything.'

She stopped chewing long enough to smile and the rough moment passed. We talked it over for a while. She was going to carry on her research in the financial Sargasso Sea of Clement's business dealings and I'd tap some sources in the PEA game, the cops, the crims, the prison system, hunting for Billie.

'I wonder who she was hiding the photo of the boy from?' I said.

'Maybe Eddie. Maybe Clement. But it means he was important to her, that's for sure. Billie doesn't take any trouble over routine things. Find him and you might find her. From the look on her face in the photo she wouldn't want to let him go, so I don't think she's in Manila.'

'Where did you meet her?'

'A flat in Liston, out past Campbelltown in case you don't know. The address I gave you. It wasn't hers. I went back and asked about her but the people there were new and not welcoming.'

'The photo could still be there. For safekeeping.'

Lou shrugged. 'More likely she took it. But you could try.'

We shook hands and left it at that. Looking for people is more interesting than serving summonses, repossessing cars and bodyguarding suits. I was glad I'd saved Lou Kramer from the clutches of Rhys Thomas.

Financially, my head was above water but not by much. The rates, phone and power bills, and insurance costs came in regularly and my income was sporadic. Still, I was a volunteer. I'd had plenty of opportunities to work for the big investigative agencies, mostly American based, and always turned them down. It wasn't the suit-wearing and the possibility that they'd be tied in to Hallburton or the FBI, although those things counted, it was the freedom to say no that I valued most. No to the political apparatchiks sniffing for dirt, no to the welfare zealots looking to entrap their 'clients'.

3

Back when I was giving lectures at Petersham TAFE in the PEA course, I told the students my first rule was: check out your client. Although I was impressed by Lou Kramer and believed her, I still followed the rule. Harry Tickener, who worked on and edited and was fired from a variety of newspapers, now runs a web-based newsletter entitled Searchlight Dot Com. His office is in Leichhardt near the Redgum Gym where I go for workouts most days. I rang Harry and told him I'd be visiting.

I went to the gym and put in a solid treadmill, free weights and machine session. The Redgum is a serious place. As Wesley Scott, the proprietor and chief trainer once said, 'This isn't a lycra gym.' Many of the members are athletes—swimmers, footballers, cricketers and basketball players—and some of us older types are ex-cops, ex-army, ex-something or other, trying to stave off the effects of age and stay flexible and strong. It works, according to the amount of time you spend at it. I'm somewhere in the middle range—the despair of the true believers who go there five or six times a week and really sweat, respected by the slackers, who attend irregularly and struggle to lift what they lifted last week.

I turned up at Harry's door a little after eleven with two large takeaway flat whites from the Bar Napoli.

Harry has stripped staff back to himself and two others and he was alone in the office when I arrived. Bald as an egg, homely and cheerful, Harry wears sneakers even with suits because he has foot trouble. Today he was in jeans and a T-shirt with his Nikes on the desk in front of him.

He mimed lifting a weight, ridiculous with his pipe-stem arms. 'Good gym?'

I clenched a fist. 'Bracing. You should try it.'

'My dad lifted a coal pick about half a million times before silicosis got him. I'm against physical work. Who was it said the best thing about being working class is that it gives you something to get out of?'

'I think it might've been Neville Wran, but your father was a funeral director.'

'So, he lifted coffins. Same thing applies. Let's have that coffee. No cake? Oh, no, you're too figure conscious these days.'

I took the lids off the coffees and handed him his, several packets of sugar and a plastic stirrer. 'I don't eat anything until the evening meal most days and then as little as I can. Gym in the morning; long walk in the afternoon or evening. Lost ten kilos. I break out from time to time, but that's the routine.'

Harry shuddered. 'Spare me. What about the grog?'

'Don't want to waste away. I take in a few calories there. Of course, as we now know, red wine's good for everything that ails you.'

I perched on the edge of his big desk; Harry poured three packets of sugar into his coffee, stirred vigorously and took an appreciative sip.

'I've got three names, Harry. Be grateful for your input on all or any.'

'What's in it for me?'

'A subscription to your newsletter.'

'You already subscribe.'

'A renewal—three year.'

'Shoot.'

'Louise Kramer. Jonas Clement. Rhys Thomas.'

'The first is doing a book on the second who employs the third.'

'Shit, Harry, I know that. I mean—'

'I know what you mean. Okay, Clement's a bit of a mystery man. Came from nowhere. I've got a suspicion it's not his original name, shall we say. At a guess, I'd bet on him being a South African or from somewhere close, like Zimbabwe.'

'Thought I twigged to an accent.'

'Right. I don't really know much about him. Bloody rich, political connections. Conservative of course.'

'Reactionary, I'd say.'

Harry grunted. 'Kramer's a bit of a handful. She wrote for me when I was running *The Clarion* and she still does bits and pieces for me. She's been around. She can research and write but tends to piss people off. Word is she got a big advance for the book. There's a story in Clement if she can suss it out. She's your client, right?'

'Yes.'

'You're doing what?'

'Looking into things for her.'

'C'mon.'

'Harry, you know I can't tell you, especially as she's writing a book. Tell you what, if she gets it done I'll try to persuade her to let you run extracts for free.'

'Her publishers'd have something to say about that, but I take the point. Now Thomas is a bad bastard. He's been banned from the racing industry for life, not allowed to look at a horse. Tough nut, but he isn't dumb.'

'I've already run up against him. He had a grip on Kramer that was likely to bruise the bone. I had to . . . cause him to stop.'

'Bad enemy to make. When was this?'

'Last night, at a Clement fund-raising party.'

'Oh, yeah, I heard about it. Absolutely no press present, meaning lots of publicity because the press speculates about who was there and who wasn't. Clement knows how to play it. Doesn't sound like your sort of gig, though.'

'I was filling in for someone.'

'How'd Lou get in?'

I shrugged.

'She's a tricky one, Cliff. Watch yourself.'

'Meaning?'

'I dunno. Her stuff was always good but I wasn't completely sure she got her info . . . ethically. Sailed close to the wind with her a few times—quotes ever so slightly doctored, questions about what was on and off the record. That kind of thing.'

We finished the coffee and the cups went into the bin. I asked Harry about Billie Marchant, mentioning that she'd been interviewed by Lou Kramer in Liston, and Eddie. He'd never heard of her and all he knew about Eddie was that he'd cashed in. 'No great loss,' he said. 'What d'you know about Liston, Cliff?'

'Heavyweight champ. Lost to Ali twice. Probably tanked the second time.'

'Very funny. It'll open your eyes. Three generations of

welfare dependents out there, with a fourth coming along.'

'Well, my grandad was on the dole when he wasn't on the wallaby, and my dad was on it in the Depression. Me too, for a bit, when the insurance company sacked me.'

'You can compare notes then with some of the people out there, but I doubt you'll find much similarity. Some of them are locked into poverty traps no one has a clue about relieving.'

'You're talking about our political masters, our elected representatives.'

Harry blew a raspberry. 'Yeah, and we're about to elect the same lot again, or worse. Stay in touch, mate. I'll hold you to that promise about the extracts if Lou gets her shit together.'

'You have doubts?'

'She always filed dead on time. What's her deadline on the book?'

'I didn't ask.'

'You should.'

'Why?'

'It puts writers under stress. Some of them spend the advance and can't get on with the book. They go for the booze or the drugs, even suicide. It's been known.'

'Sounds like you know.'

'Sort of. I've been trying to write a novel for years. Can't crack it.' Harry waved his hand at the computer and other professional material in the room. 'Lucky I've got this. Haven't you ever tried to do something and couldn't make it, Cliff?'

'Sure. Tried to clear six feet in the high jump. Five eleven and a half was fine but I knocked the bar off every time at six feet.'

'So, what did you do?'

'Changed to the long jump.'

'And?'

'Couldn't clear sixteen feet.'

'Same thing, mental barrier. So?'

'Went surfing. I could stand up on the board and if I fell off it didn't matter.'

'Ask her.'

Perhaps by nature, certainly by experience and habit, private enquiry agents are suspicious and mistrustful. But some friendships take and hold and I had one going back quite a way with Bob Armstrong. Bob had eventually yielded to the blandishments of one of the corporations and become a security consultant and functionary within its organisation, but before that he'd been a keen and successful independent operator. I rang him, told him I wanted to talk about a former colleague, and we agreed to meet for a drink at six in Balmain.

'In the glorious smoke-free pub where you can breathe the air and taste the beer,' he said.

'Didn't know there was one.'

He named it. The day heated up considerably and I did a few routine things, like returning the dinner suit to the hirer, depositing Lou Kramer's cheque and paying a few bills before heading to the Dawn Fraser baths at four thirty for a pre-drink and work swim. The baths have gone through a few changes over the years but not many. The water's better now than a few years ago when the harbour around Balmain was very sludgy. I paid for a locker and stripped, wrapped my mobile in the towel and went out on the boards.

There's something Old Sydney, in the true sense, that I like about the place. I remember the photo of poor Les Darcy in his trunks with the kids at the Manly baths, ninety years back. He looked as hard as a rock and ready to take on any middleweight on the planet. That image was in my head as I walked towards a clear spot. The way it is with me when a case is on hand, I could hear the voices of the people I'd spoken to inside my head. *This is my shot,* I heard Lou Kramer saying. Les never got his shot. Should have.

I tucked my towel and thongs into a corner, dived in and swam a few lengths. The water was choppy because a light wind had sprung up. I enjoyed the swim, pulled myself out and headed for the towel. The mobile chirped and I answered it with water still in my ears. I could scarcely make out the voice.

'Can't hear you. Hang on. I have to clear water from my ears. Okay. Who is it?'

'It's Lou Kramer. Why've you got water in your ears?'

'I've been swimming.'

'Swimming!'

'Healthy mind in a healthy body. What's up?'

'I wanted to tell you not to deposit that cheque just yet.'

'I've already deposited it. Paid extra for quick clearance.'

'Shit, it'll bounce. I'm sorry. I have to move some money around.'

'You're not filling me with confidence.'

'It'll be fine in a day or so. Just re-present it. I'll pay the fee.'

'I've got a question for you. What's your deadline for the book?'

'Why d'you ask?'

'Just curious.'

'None of your bloody business. Sorry again about the cheque.'

She rang off. I thought a better rule than check on your client might be check on your client's bank balance.

Bob Armstrong once attempted to work up a PEA trade union of a sort but he had no luck. I played along for a while until it was clear there was no possibility of such a bunch of individuals with highly diversified lifestyles, values and politics ever cohering. Still, Bob stayed in touch with others in the profession as a matter of principle and occasionally organised a whip-round when someone fell on hard times.

The Red Unicorn hotel used to be a bit of a bloodhouse like many of the pubs in Balmain. Again like many, it gentrified along with the area itself, so that it had a bistro and sold boutique beers. TAB facility and a bank of pokies, but not too many. There were signs advertising live music two nights a week and a trivia competition. All the hallmarks of the trendy twenty-first century pub. The smoke-free rule was its newest pitch at the high disposable income crowd. Didn't worry me: I'd given up the rollies long ago. The last cigarette I'd lit in a moment of stress after years of abstinence tasted like old dog blanket and I knew I was cured. Bob, another quitter, had been a ferocious smoker and was still a keen drinker. The Unicorn was an obvious choice for a meeting.

Bob was at the bar when I arrived. I hadn't laid eyes on him since he'd gone corporate and seeing him in a suit was a shock. I was in my usual late spring to early summer uniform of drill slacks, cotton shirt and beat-up linen jacket. Bob was working on a schooner and had a middy sitting beside it. He looked at his watch as I approached.

'Dead on time. Knew you would be so I ordered you a beer.'

I toasted him with it. 'Thanks.' I touched the lapel of his jacket. 'Nice suit. Doing well, Bob?'

'I have to say I am. No overheads, car in the package, health insurance . . .'

'I could do with that.'

'But not with the rest of it, eh, Cliff?'

'A dinosaur?'

'Not quite, but an endangered species, that's for sure. This former colleague is . . . ?'

I looked around before answering. The nearest drinker was three or four stools away and the barman was well out of hearing. Old habit—names spoken aloud in public can attract attention. 'Was Eddie Flannery.'

'Poor Eddie. Went down a long flight of stone steps. Possible suicide but probably pissed.'

'I heard he was murdered.'

'Did you now? That wasn't the coroner's opinion. Accidental death.'

'I missed all this. When did it happen?'

'A few months ago.'

'Precisely when?'

Bob, who'd put on weight since I'd last seen him, stroked the beginnings of a jowl and took a long pull on his schooner. 'Eight weeks, give or take a day or two. That's the inquest. The death was about six weeks earlier. Can't be more exact than that. I went to the funeral. It was pissing down.'

I finished the middy and signalled to the barman.

'That's as it should be. It must've been when I was in Queensland.'

'None of it made much of a splash.'

'Was Billie Marchant there?'

'Sure was. Very fetching in black in a Barbara Stanwyck sort of way, if you get me. What's this about, Cliff?'

I told him as much as I felt entitled to. He didn't know about Eddie's association with Clement and when that name came up he seemed to run dry of information, even though he had a fair amount of alcohol inside him. So did I, and I was facing a walk home to Glebe.

'Why do I get the feeling you're closing up on me, Bob?'

Bob suddenly looked as if he'd like a cigarette. Instead, he started to shred his coaster. The fingers that used to be nicotine-stained with bitten-down nails were manicured but nervous. 'Clement's a client of the firm I'm with.'

'Then you should be a mine of information about him.'

He shook his head. 'Not a chance.'

'Bad guy is he?'

'You won't get another word out of me. In fact, I'm going. Sorry, Cliff.'

He was halfway off his stool. I grabbed his arm. Felt the quality of the material of his jacket. 'You've been helpful. I'll tell anyone who asks.'

'Fuck, no. I wasn't here.'

He pulled free and left quickly. Hadn't even finished his drink. I topped mine up with what he'd left and went into the bistro with the two-thirds full glass. I ordered a steak and salad, no fries, and eked the drink out over the meal. Bob Armstrong had softened up since his days as an independent, but he'd never been short on guts and the genuine fear in his attitude surprised me. It sounded as though he wouldn't mention our meeting to anyone at his place of business, but I couldn't be sure. Anyway, I was glad I hadn't talked about Billie's kid.

4

It was a good night for a walk and a think, and it's always good to avoid being breathalysed. The car was safely parked and locked and there wasn't anything worth stealing in it. If someone wanted my sweaty gym gear and salty swimmers they were welcome. I was due for new stuff anyway.

At one time, Wednesday would have been an unusual night for a party like the one at Clement's, but these days corporate types work seven days a week and have clocks around them set to London, Tokyo and New York time and a week has taken on an entirely different shape. For us lesser mortals, Thursday still means late night shopping and activity beyond the usual in the streets. I walked down Darling Street to Victoria Road and negotiated my way down to pick up the Crescent. I thought about cutting through Jubilee Park but decided against it. People do private things there at night and I respect their privacy. The Wigram Road hill is a good calf muscle stretcher and I was thinking I might reward myself for my virtue by having a quick one at the Toxteth hotel.

I tried to remember when I'd last been in Campbelltown and couldn't. I knew I'd never been to its outer suburbs and decided I'd do a web search on Liston before I went out there. Couldn't hurt. I was halfway up the hill when I became aware of something unusual. It wasn't much—a feeling that a car light behind me wasn't quite right, a half-heard idling car motor. I didn't turn round but my senses were alerted and before I got to Glebe Point Road I knew there was a car, hanging back, slowing, letting others pass, following me.

I stepped up the pace, crossed over Wigram Road and used the pedestrian crossing over Glebe Point Road. Then I walked briskly past the couple of trendy shops and into the Toxteth. If someone wanted to talk to me they could do it here. If they wanted to do something else they could whistle for it. This was my turf, and I could make it home in ways only someone who'd lived here for twenty years would know.

I went in by the Ferry Road door through the pool area with its swanky blue baize tables. Three of them. Two youngsters, looking barely old enough to be in the place, were smoking, drinking and knocking the balls about—misspending their youth and enjoying it. I went into the bar where there were padded chairs and settees, plus stools and classy framed sporting prints on the walls. I bought a scotch and went back to watch the pool players. A mistake. Three men in suits entered the pub—Rhys Thomas and two others, both very big.

They moved quickly and purposefully, Thomas blocking the Ferry Road door to the street and one of the biggies standing in the wide opening between the pool area and the bar. It's wide, but if he'd spread his arms he could just about have covered the distance.

I put my glass down, and picked up a cue and a ball. The one wearing the smartest suit took two fifties from his wallet, handed one to each of the kids and gestured with his thumb.

'Out!'

They left. He replaced Thomas by the Ferry Road door and Thomas advanced towards me. I moved to put a table between myself and him.

'You made me look foolish in front of my employer, Hardy,' Thomas said.

I mimed being hard of hearing. 'What was that?'

It threw him for a second and gave me a chance to snap the cue under my foot, making it a more dangerous weapon.

'I said you made me look foolish in front of my employer.'

'I heard you,' I said. 'It wasn't hard.'

He advanced and I poked the jagged end of the cue at him. 'Back off. I could take out an eye.'

He retreated but the other man didn't. Anticipating my move, he got close enough to try a karate kick to my leg. I just managed to swing the cue back and down. I don't know anything about karate, but in the movies they always hit the right spot. He didn't. The cue got him squarely on the shin. He yelped and swore and bent double. Points to me, but it gave Thomas his chance. He closed in and swung a punch into my groin. End of story. The pain shot through me upwards, downwards and sideways. I dropped the cue and went into a protective crouch. He brought his knee up, caught me on the forehead and I felt my brain swim and my vision slide away.

'Jesus, man,' I heard one of the suits say. 'That was sweet.'

I was still conscious and, dimly, thought it wasn't nearly enough if Thomas was fair dinkum. Then I realised that my blurred vision was due to blood flowing down into my eyes. Not trickling, flowing.

'I think he's got the message, Rhys. Let's go before you get blood all over yourself.'

I propped myself up against the leg of the table and drew in several deep breaths. The pain in my groin was bad but I'd had worse from low blows in the ring and a rifle butt in army training. The trick is to suck in air and think of higher things. I wasn't too worried about the blood because I knew what had happened. Thomas's hard, bony knee had split the scar tissue I have over my right eye, a memento of my amateur boxing career. We didn't always wear protective headgear then. I have sharp eyebrow ridges, like Jimmy Carruthers, and, as he did, I bleed there like a stuck pig. It'd look worse than it was. Cautiously, I raised my right arm and wiped at the spot.

'Christ, mate. Are you all right?'

One of the drinkers had drifted in from the bar. I must've been quite a sight.

'This is like the old days,' he said. 'Here.'

He closed my hand around the drink I'd abandoned. I gave my forehead and eyes another wipe and my vision cleared. Massive dry-cleaning bill but not much more damage. I drank the scotch.

'Thanks. Little misunderstanding.'

He was half drunk, fat and good-natured. 'Coppers come around this time of night. Better get yourself cleaned up.'

Most of the blood had soaked into my jacket; my shirt was dark so the blood on it didn't show. I pulled myself up, took off the jacket after finding some tissues in a pocket. I pressed them against the eyebrow cut and went through to the toilet without attracting any attention. The face in the mirror looked like mine but it had aged a bit more than it should have in the last half-hour. I ran the water, used most of the paper towels available to clean up as best I could. I'd need ice for the swelling, a warm bath for the sore balls and a caustic stick for the cut. All available at home a few hundred metres away. Over the years, I'd spent so much money in the Toxteth I didn't feel I had to compensate them for the broken cue.

It took me three times longer than usual to get home from the pub and I was glad none of my neighbours saw me in such a mess. The cut had opened wide again and I was bloody from my head to my feet. I stripped off, had a shower and sat for a while in a shallow bath. I used the caustic stick to stop the bleeding. The skin above the eyebrow had been cut and stitched several times. These days they use some kind of clip that doesn't promote scar tissue, but not in my time. Eventually the blood stopped seeping, but it'd be a while before the swelling went down and the scab came away. Till then, I was going to look like someone who'd been in a fight and I hadn't even landed a punch.

I made a pot of coffee and spiked a big mug of it with brandy. I had three painkillers and by the time I was halfway through the second spiked coffee I was feeling solid enough to do some thinking. I ran my mind back over the encounter in the pub and a few things about it struck me as strange. Rhys Thomas could obviously handle himself, so why would he need two heavies in support? I'd got him to repeat his grievance because there seemed to be something almost rehearsed about it as it came out the first time, and even more so the second. I was searching for a lead on the guy with the money and it came to me. He bore a strong resemblance to Jonas Clement. A son? And, although it's hard to tell from one word, and one phrase, the way he pronounced 'Out!' and his use of 'man' had a South African touch to them.

If I was right in my guesses, all that put the pub incident in a very different light. Clement's son wouldn't have gone along to support Thomas on a personal affront. More likely he was doing what his dad wanted him to do, which was put the frighteners on me. That meant he knew about my connection with Louise Kramer and was sufficiently worried about it to take some pretty crude action. I called Lou's home and mobile numbers and got the voicemail. I left a message sketching in a few of my suspicions and suggesting that we get together urgently. Nothing more to be done tonight.

I went to bed with my coffee and brandy and paracetamol buzz with one comforting thought. There hadn't been time for Bob Armstrong to alert anyone to my interest in Clement and activate the Thomas heavy brigade. That still left the question of how, when and why Clement came to think me worthy of his plutocratic attention.

Lou Kramer rang me before eight the next morning. She said she was using some flexi-time she'd racked up before she went on to a part-time contract to work at home and was too busy to meet me anywhere. She asked me to come to her flat. No harm in sussing out the client's residence. I got a taxi to Balmain and picked up the car. Untouched. I parked with dubious legality, walked a block, and buzzed at the door of the newly and expensively renovated old building in Surry Hills. It stood across from Ward Park, named after Eddie Ward, 'the firebrand of East Sydney', a hero of my father's. Fewer of Eddie's kind of voters around here now.

'The Surrey Apartments'— six floors and from the top there'd be a great view of the city whichever way you looked.

'Push, Cliff. Fifth floor.' I pushed and the door released. The lift was smooth and quick and she was standing with the door open when I got there.

'Jesus Christ, you just said you'd been knocked about a bit.'

'It's not as bad as it looks.'

She beckoned me in and kept staring at my battered face. 'That reminds me of that joke about Wagner—his music's not as bad as it sounds. Can you see out of that eye?'

'Sure. So this's what you pay the big mortgage on? Pretty nice.'

'Location, location, location.'

The apartment had a short, wide hallway giving on to a big, light, airy living room with several rooms leading off it. The windows ran from waist high almost to the ceiling and the outlook was to the east. I'm always amazed to see how many trees there really are in Sydney. The sky was cloudy and visibility wasn't good but I suspected there'd be a view of water on a clear day. The room had a good lived-in feel, with books, magazines, CDs and DVDs not put away where they belonged. What looked like the day's broadsheets lay around, haphazardly folded open.

At her invitation I sat near a low table on a comfortable chair and she brought in coffee. She glanced at her watch as she set the tray down.

'I won't keep you long.'

'Sorry. It's just that I have to make the most of this time for my own work.'

'Understood.'

She wore loose pants, sandals and a denim shirt. The top of a packet of her anti-smoking gum peeked from the breast pocket. No makeup, hair barely combed. Working, and not bothering about anything else.

'I'll get to the point,' I said. 'Have you told anyone about hiring me?'

'Why?'

Not the answer I'd hoped for. 'Because I think Clement was behind the attack on me. There was more to it than just Thomas getting even. By the way, does Clement have a son?'

'Yes, big lump of a lad, a nasty type, did a bit of mercenary work—Jonas Junior.'

'He was there last night. More or less in control. You haven't answered my question, Lou.'

'I told someone, yes.'

'Who?'

'I can't tell you.'

I drank some coffee and looked at her. She drank and didn't look at me. 'Why not?' I said.

'I'm not supposed to be seeing him. He's married and all that.'

'You think I'd spill it to "Stay in Touch"?'

She shook her head. 'Of course not. It's just that I promised him I wouldn't tell anyone. Look, Cliff, I trust him. He wouldn't . . .'

'Does he have any connection with Clement?'

'I . . . I'm not sure.'

'C'mon, Lou.'

She wasn't the kind of woman you could push. She flared. 'Do you want to back out?'

I looked around the room again. It had the appearance of a journalist's place—lots of print, up-to-date media machines, a couple of Whiteley prints and Dupain's 'The Sunbather' on the walls. I finished my coffee and stood.

'Let me see your workroom.'

'Shit, why?'

'Indulge me.'

She shrugged and pointed to a half-open door. I went into a room with the blind drawn. Bookshelves, filing cabinets and a big pine table with an iMac computer, printer, scanner and thumb drive lit by a desk lamp. The surface was awash with scribbled notes on post-its, notepads covered with scrawled handwriting, pens and pencils. Squinting in the dim light, I browsed the bookshelves. The Paul Barry best-selling jobs on Bond and Packer; Christine Wallace on Germaine Greer; D'Alpuget on Hawke; Watson on Keating; Knightley's *A Hack's Progress;* some Richard Hall and a full shelf on African travel, politics and economics. And much else—Bernard Levin, Clive James, David Leich, Paul Theroux, and Bob Ellis. She was a journalism junkie, with a yen to travel.

I turned back to see her standing in the doorway. She opened her hands and did a perfect imitation of the guy in the beer commercial who freaks out his girlfriend in the spa.

'What?'

I grinned. 'Nothing. What you read you are.'

'Another stolen line.'

'Right. I don't think I'm getting a fair shake here. Your cheque's going to bounce—'

'It'll clear tomorrow.'

I ignored her. 'You won't tell me your deadline; you say Eddie was murdered but the official version is it was an accident; you won't name your mystery man . . .'

'I'm sorry.'

'Tell me the deadline.'

'Oh, all right. I've got three months to finish the bloody thing and I'm battling to make it, especially if . . .'

'You don't find Billie.'

'Yes. Are you pulling out?'

'No,' I said. 'It's personal now.'

5

I told Lou to be careful about where she went and the company she kept. If my suspicion that Clement had tried to frighten me off was right, he wouldn't be beyond renewing his attacks on her. Except that I was an independent operator in a not-highly-regarded profession and she was in the media, the new aristocracy.

'I go from here to the office and back as it suits me and them. That's it,' she said. 'I phone out for groceries, grog and pizza.'

'What about when you meet up with Mr X?'

'Oh, I'd be safe enough with him.'

I left and went to the gym for the lightest of workouts and a long soak in the spa. Back in the office I worked the Internet and the phone. I discovered that Liston was officially one of the thirty most disadvantaged postcodes in the country according to a sociological survey. The suburb had been named after a local farm and had become a dumping ground for battlers needing Department of Housing help in the eighties. Back then, it was at a distance from Campbelltown—out of sight and mind. It had a very high level of unemployment and welfare dependency and a considerable Aboriginal population.

I had contacts in the parole system and social services and from some of them I got a picture of how the place had changed in recent years.

Terri Boxall, a parole officer, said, 'It was a shithole to start with. One of those good ideas gone wrong. They built the houses cheek by jowl all facing this big open parkland with virtually no private space per house. The dead-end kids turned the open space into no-go areas and the rest of the people huddled inside by the tele drinking and producing more dead-end kids.'

'You imply it's got better.'

'It sure has. The Department turned the houses around—remodelled them so they faced away and knocked some down so there was some private space.'

'I can't imagine a government department being that imaginative. Worked, did it?'

'To an extent, but the big thing was the introduction of the Islanders.'

That got my attention. 'Islanders?'

'Samoans, Tongans, Fijians. They sorted out the car thieves, burglars and yahoos. They're churchy, you know? Law-abiding, despite their problems.'

'When was this, Terri?'

'It's been progressive. Probably started eight, ten years ago.'

'That could fit.'

'What's your interest, Cliff?'

'I'm looking for a woman named Billie Marchant. Ever heard the name?'

'Sorry, no.'

'I know she's got friends out there, and she's got a kid and I'm assuming she's in touch with him. I don't know how old he is—maybe fifteen, maybe more. In a photo he looks to be black.'

'What's his name? Are they in your kind of trouble?'

'No, not directly. I just might be able to help them. Hard to say at this point. I don't know his name.'

'Good luck. Tell you what, there's a sort of community protection set-up there. I've got a few . . . clients in Liston and these people help me keep tabs on them from time to time.'

'Community protection?'

'Civil rights fundamentalists might call it vigilantism. I wouldn't. Have a word with John Manuma. Mention my name.'

'Got a phone number?'

'He wouldn't be interested in talking to you on the phone, Cliff. You'd have to front him, face to face, as it were.'

'As it were?'

'He's a Samoan, two hundred centimetres or thereabouts.'

'That tops me by a fair bit. Shouldn't be hard to spot.'

Terri told me that the community protection office was a shopfront in Liston's only commercial centre and that it was staffed by volunteers and open seven days a week, so Saturday wasn't going to be a problem. I wasn't going out there today because tonight I was going to keep an eye on Lou Kramer, hoping to find out who her Mr X was. She was playing her game by her own rules, and in mine you just can't be too careful.

After a quiet afternoon, I was in my car at 6 pm equipped with field glasses and a camera, stationed across the way from the entrance to the Surrey Apartments. Lovers get together on Friday nights if they possibly can, for however short a time. Husbands tell their wives they have to work late cleaning their desks; working wives do the same. For both sexes there's the excuse of a drink with the fellow workers. Just the one.

I came into the business as the no-fault divorce laws were taking away work from private investigators. One or two of what were called 'Brownie and bedsheets' cases and it was all over. As a beneficiary of no-fault divorce myself I wasn't sorry, but it took some zip out of the profession, like the end of the Cold War did out of spying. This was about the closest I'd been to it since those days.

I was still there at 8 pm with no sign of Lou or a likely candidate for her lover. The few men who'd arrived had either been in the company of other men or women or, in the cases of the two who arrived alone, and whom I photographed, they left again within a few minutes, barely time to have given Lou a peck on the cheek.

At about eight thirty a silver BMW circled the block searching for a park. The driver made two circuits before a space opened up and he slid the car into it. He got out and approached the apartment building, passing within thirty metres of me. The camera could cope with the dim light and I got a good shot of him in profile. For a nasty split second I thought something had alerted him to my presence because he turned full face towards me, but he was only looking at a skateboarder who'd jumped a gutter with a clatter and a bang and was whizzing along the footpath. I didn't need another picture because I'd seen him before. He was the man at the party who'd been cynical about the pro-Americanism and speaking style of Jonas Clement.

He went into the building. I got out of my car and walked past his, noting the registration number. I was back behind the wheel when Lou and the BMW driver came out. She was dressed pretty much the way she had been at the party. He was in a business suit, no tie. Probably passed for casual with him. Out of the tailored dinner suit, with his jacket open, he looked less impressive than he had at the party. He was tall and spindly, but carrying ten kilos he didn't need, mostly around the middle, also around his face and neck. He had thin, dark hair slicked down and a bustling walk. Lou held on to his arm as if he might get away. They stood on the footpath for a few minutes until a taxi pulled up. He handed her gallantly into the passenger side back seat, then went around and got in beside her. I started my engine, waited, U-turned and followed the taxi.

The cab cruised down Devonshire Street, negotiated the lights at Eddy Avenue and took George until it turned off towards Darling Harbour. It was a slow run through heavy traffic and easy to keep it in sight. It pulled up outside the Malaya restaurant at King Street Wharf and the happy couple went inside. Must have had a reservation because the place is packed most of the time and especially for dinner on Friday night. I could've gone a prawn sambal myself but I wouldn't have got a seat and there was nowhere to park. How the other half lives.

I drove back and found a semi-legal parking place in Chinatown. A short walk and I was at my favourite Sydney restaurant—the Superbowl in Goulburn Street. No problem for a single diner here as long as he's ready to share a table. I was and got a seat at a table with a Chinese couple who ignored me. As always, the clientele was ninety-five per cent Asian which, to my mind, is the best indication that the food is good. The service is lightning fast as the object is to move people through as quickly as possible and that's always fine by me if I'm on my own.

I had what I always have—shredded chicken with salty fish in fried rice and a big glass of the house white. I ate as much as I could manage of the perfectly cooked and blended meal and left the rest reluctantly. In and out in just under an hour and twenty dollars. I eat there as often as I can, perhaps twice a month. The waiters must know me but they never acknowledge that they've seen me before. I like that.

Anticipating that Lou and Mr X would take longer over their meal, I wandered up George Street, checked out what was on at the movies, had a coffee. Still, I was back in Surry Hills too early and had to kick my heels for a while until the taxi pulled up. Lou and her date stood outside the apartment building for a few minutes. She gesticulated; he shook his head. He leaned down to kiss her and she stepped back, then relented and they kissed briefly. She turned away quickly and headed for the security buttons. He heaved a theatrical sigh, crossed the street and used his remote to unlock the Beemer.

Very interesting, I thought, but what it meant I had no idea. I considered following him to wherever he was going, but decided against it. A light rain was falling and I wouldn't have been able to keep pace with the BMW if he decided to open it up. Besides, a bit of voyeurism goes a long way with me and I had enough on him. By office hours on Monday I'd know who he was and where he lived.

Late night news on TV. The election campaign was in its fourth week of six, but it was hard to get excited about it.

The ALP had long ago put Karl Marx in mothballs and embraced Milton Friedman or one of his disciples. The conservatives were continually reassuring us that we were safe and secure, meaning that our houses and investments were—that is, as long as you had a house and investments. If you didn't *you* were insecure and it was probably your fault. It certainly wasn't theirs.

Pollies in suits, men and women, went around the supermarkets and malls and appeared on television pretending to be ordinary people, when they probably couldn't tell you the price of a litre of milk or what it cost to register a Toyota Corolla. Not within a bull's roar.

Time was when I followed politics and listened to what the players had to say to see who made the most sense. Now, it all sounded scripted and rehearsed and came out no better than white noise. Both sides made wild promises about what they'd do with our taxes; the side that lost wouldn't have to honour them and the side that won would find ways to renege. I'd voted left all my life, and this time I was considering trying something witty as an informal vote—that's if I was free on the Saturday.

It's fifty kilometres south-west from Sydney to Campbelltown and a few more north of that to Liston. I made the drive through light traffic on a warm Saturday morning. On a non-holiday weekend, with the football season finished and no other major sporting events on, the traffic is local in all directions and I made good time. It wasn't an area I was very familiar with. The web search had told me there were 150 000 people in Campbelltown and the number was going up all the time. I knew that some of those people went south over the escarpment down to the Illawarra coast for their holidays and that many of them had never been to Sydney. There were pockets of affluence and stretches of poverty, 'aspirational' voters and battlers, a university and the 'legend of Fisher's ghost'—the story from colonial days of the ghost of a murdered man named Fisher manifesting itself and pointing the way to where the body had been deposited. That led to the murderer who was convicted and necked. It was about time I got better acquainted with the place.

I drove the Hume Highway to St Andrews and worked my way to Liston via secondary roads. There was still a lot of open land around Glenfield and the Ingleburn military establishment, but all the area to the south was filling up fast.

At first glance, Liston didn't look too bad. For one thing the land rose and fell so that the dreary flatness that characterises a lot of the outer suburbs didn't apply. As Terri had said, there was a big open parkland and recreational space in the centre of the area and although the schools featured mainly demountable buildings, that isn't uncommon from Bermagui to Byron Bay. I drove around for a while to get the feel of the place and some of the realities became clear. The houses were clustered close together and their construction had been made with economy chiefly in mind. The early settlers knew how to build for this climate—overhanging eaves, wide verandahs. But such things are expensive and Liston's planners had cut shade and outdoor living area to the bone.

A good many of the residents had tried their best by planting trees and contriving add-ons of one kind or another but the trees mostly hadn't flourished, and the add-ons had been pressed into service as carports and storage areas. There were unroadworthy cars gathering weeds in a good many of the minuscule front yards and some examples of that distinctive feature of disadvantage—broken furniture left out in the open.

The picture wasn't altogether grim though. Some of the closely packed houses had small but well-tended gardens and what looked to my ignorant eye to be vegetable and herb plots. I drove the perimeter and noted the signs of a major up-market development named 'Shetland Hills' taking shape to the west of Liston. A major road separated the development from Liston and all the residents of Shetland Hills would be able to see of their neighbours were faded colourbond fences. A few towering Shetland structures were up already and I drove back to the centre of Liston with a new perspective. A lot of the houses looked okay, but how many people lived in them?

The bus shelters were heavily graffitied and a good few of the graffitists were hanging about—loose clothes, big sneakers, caps reversed. Many of them had dark faces and some had the big, bulky Polynesian build. There were a lot of young children in the streets and a lot of women pushing prams. Another sign of disadvantage—almost half of the women and children were fat.

Nobody paid me much attention as I wandered around: too occupied with their own concerns. I strolled across some scruffy parkland to a low brick building where there seemed to be some activity and sound. As I got closer I could hear the singing. It had that tuneful, plaintive note I'd heard in Fiji and New Caledonia in my few Pacific sojourns.

I went as close as I could without intruding and saw that the hall inside was packed with Islanders, men, women and children, being led in song by one of their own. Unlike them, he was wearing smart clothes that didn't conceal that he was enormously fat. Sweat glistened on his bald head, and when he raised his arms I could see dark patches. At this rate his suit was going to need dry-cleaning after every singsong.

When you hear the singing in the islands, you seem to be able to catch the sound of the sea on the reef and the wind in the palm trees. Not here. All the cadences were of the Pacific, but the words were from a militant Christian hymn, promising salvation for the faithful and misery for sinners. It reminded me of the Methodist Sunday school my father had vainly tried to make me attend. I went once, and every time thereafter nicked off to the beach and spent the collection plate money on lollies.

The commercial hub of Liston was a long, low-slung building on the edge of the open space fronted by a car park that wouldn't have held fifty cars. I parked and walked down steps to the building that resembled an extra long and wide Nissan hut partitioned to form shops. There was a liquor outlet at the east end but it was shut and heavily padlocked. A sign warned that alcohol was not permitted to be consumed on the premises or in the adjacent area. At the other end was a health centre where about twenty people were congregated. I could hear coughing and babies crying.

The shopping precinct boasted a takeaway food shop, a video store, a newsagent, a supermarket and a couple of small shops that looked like Pacific island trade stores with goods piled up and hanging as if there was no real expectation of them being sold. I could smell cooking going on at the back of one of these shops. None of the shops were doing much business. There was a lot of litter and a carpet of cigarette butts on the cement surrounds.

The community protection office was next to the supermarket. The window was covered with notices—appointment times for a JP, Crime Stoppers and Neighbourhood Watch stickers, advertisements for alternative medicines, whacko therapies of different kinds and religious attractions. The glass in the window was clean and the area in front of the office had recently been thoroughly swept. Looking through the open door I saw two desks with people behind them and someone on a chair in front of each. There were a few more people in the room waiting their turn. I went in and leaned against the wall. There were noticeboards carrying flyers for community meetings, garage sales and work wanted. On one board three familiar documents jumped out at me—the standard police notice with a photograph of a missing person. Two females, one male, ages from twelve to fifteen. The notices weren't new.

Both people behind the desk were Islanders, a woman and a man. The man fitted the description of John Manuma that Terri Boxall had given me. He was talking in a low voice to another Islander. I couldn't hear what he was saying but it didn't matter because he wasn't speaking English. The woman was dealing with a white woman and they appeared to be discussing the advisability or otherwise of an AVO. Of the three other people waiting in the room, two were dark; I made it an even split. With my olive skin darkened by the sun, my nose flattened by boxing and professional hazards and my scarred eyebrows, I'd often been taken for Aboriginal. Not by Kooris, though.

The woman became free after dealing with three clients quickly, and beckoned to me.

'Thanks,' I said. 'But if that's Mr Manuma I have business specifically with him.'

The big man glanced up quickly but went on with what he was saying.

'Okay,' the woman said and waved a man who'd come in after me forward.

Raised voices and the sound of a scuffle brought Manuma to his feet. He was a giant, over 200 centimetres and heavy in the upper body and legs. He strode through the door and I moved after him to watch. Two men, one white, one black, were shouting abuse at each other while a dark woman with two clinging children stood by looking anxious. A white woman was egging the black man on.

'Fuckin' do 'im, Archie,' she yelled. 'Fuckin' cunt.'

Archie lurched forward, clearly not sober, and threw a punch the other man easily avoided. Manuma shouted something and an Islander woman emerged from one of the shops, clapped her hand over the white woman's mouth and wrestled her away. Manuma grabbed both men by their long hair, lifted them from the ground and brought their heads together. It's not something you see very often, if ever. The effect on both of being treated so contemptuously was more shocking than painful. The fight went out of them and they stumbled away in different directions.

It surprised me that no crowd had gathered. Evidently such conflicts were a common occurrence and Manuma's summary justice not unusual. Nevertheless, the incident prompted a feeling of tension and I noticed that the outnumbered whites waiting outside at the medical centre moved slightly away from the dark people.

Manuma returned to his seat and to his discussion with his client as if nothing had happened. When he was free he nodded at me and I took a seat. 'John Manuma,' he said without offering to shake hands. 'What can I do for you, Mr Hardy?'

6

'Terri Boxall phoned me about you.'

Now we shook hands. As well as being taller than Terri had said, he had considerably more than a hundred kilos with it. He wasn't particularly friendly and his big, broad face wore a sceptical look as I gave him a version of the story.

'Lot of people out here, brother. Lot of coming and going.'

I read off the address where Lou had talked to Billie Marchant. I'd driven past it—indistinguishable from dozens of others, perhaps a bit more rundown looking than most. 'D'you know the people there now?'

He shook his massive head. 'Nothing comes to mind.'

'Terri said she thought you'd be helpful.'

'She shouldn't have said that without me hearing your story first.'

'You've heard it now.'

'Yes, and I reckon it's a lot of nothing. I don't think there's anything here for you, Mr Hardy.'

He gave me a hard stare, then looked over my head at whoever was next in line. Not hard for him to do; sitting down, he was bigger than me in every way. His hands, on the paper-strewn desk, were the colour of teak and the size of shovel blades. He oozed impatience and aggression, and the combination lifted me out of the chair as if a hook had taken me by the collar and swung me aside. It was a new experience—being dismissed with a curiously strong element of indifference. I left the room struggling to maintain dignity.

I learned long ago not to expect things always to turn out well, but a knock-back of this intensity took me by surprise. I wandered out into the sunshine and stumped up the steps to the car park. I hadn't replaced my sunglasses and was slow to adjust to the bright light and was almost run down by a cruising police car. I stepped back just in time and swore. An Islander woman standing nearby gave me a dirty look. All in all, it wasn't a good start to my work in Liston.

I went back down to the shopping area and took another look at the liquor store. Still closed. I went into one of the all-purpose shops where three immense Polynesian women were sitting chatting while cooking something on a portable stove.

'Excuse me,' I said, 'can you tell me when the bottle shop opens?'

'Closed,' one woman said.

'I know, but when will it be open?'

'Closed for good.'

'Why?'

She shrugged and they went on talking as if the subject was of no interest. What they were cooking smelled delicious, but the shop sold vegetables, clothes, shoes and other things that meant health regulations forbade food preparation. They didn't look concerned and it seemed that Liston was in some ways a law unto itself.

I left the shop and a man approached me with a smile on his face, the first smile I'd seen there. Tall, he was Aboriginal, built on a much smaller scale than the Islanders. In his late teens at a guess, and to judge from his clothes—a threadbare T-shirt, dirty jeans and thongs—not doing too well.

'Think I can help you, brother,' he said.

'How's that?'

'I was in the office when you was talking to Johnny. I know who lives there.'

'Where?'

'At that address you said. And I know the woman you was talking about. I mean, I seen her.'

'Are you sure?'

He nodded his head and his ill-kept dreads bounced. I looked closely at him. Despite the signs of poverty, he didn't appear to be mentally adrift, drunk or drug-damaged. His eyes were clear and his body was lean but not withered.

'All right,' I said. 'You are?'

'Tommy.'

'My name's Cliff Hardy. You heard what I'm here for. What're you suggesting, Tommy?'

He smiled again and rubbed his thumb and forefinger together in the universal gesture. 'You want to talk to the chick, I can help.'

'Chick?'

'Girl, whatever. Lives there with her kids.'

'Can you get me inside the house?'

'I reckon, yeah.'

'And about the woman?'

'What about the money, brother?'

'Is there an ATM around here?'

'Newsagent got one.'

'Wait here.'

I drew out five hundred dollars. No telling how useful Tommy might be, or his rates. I bought a diet coke and changed one of the fifties so I'd have smaller chips to play with. Tommy was standing more or less where I'd left him.

'Gotta smoke?'

I handed him a twenty. 'Get yourself some and I'll see you by the blue Falcon in the car park. The dirty one with the dings.'

He grinned, took the money and loped away. I popped the can and took a drink. Things were looking up, maybe. Tommy returned with a cigarette in his mouth and another tucked behind his ear. I stuffed the can into an overflowing bin. We got into the car and drove to the address I'd looked at before. It was one of the more hard-bitten of the houses with no attempt made in the garden, a mattress leaking stuffing on the front porch and a broken swing rusting in the side yard. Lou had described the room where she'd interviewed Billie and the furniture, including the drawer where she'd seen the photograph. I pulled up two doors away.

'Here's the deal,' I said. 'I want to go in and look at a particular piece of furniture and ask about this woman I'm trying to locate.'

Tommy blew smoke. 'Got you.'

'Fifty for you, a hundred for whoever's there.'

'Hey, why?'

'I'm invading their home. You're just a go-between.'

He thought about it as he finished his cigarette. He lit

the one from behind his ear from the butt, then dropped the butt through the car window. 'Okay. Stay here and I'll see what gives.'

He slipped out, slammed the door, and crossed the street, stepped through the open gate and went up the path to the door of the house. I kept my eye on him as I got out and went around to put my foot on the smouldering butt. I leaned against the car and was grateful for the sunglasses because the sun was high and bright and my battered eye still hurt a bit. The door to the house opened and a woman stood there. She had a baby on her hip and a toddler peeked around her legs at the caller. Tommy started talking and offered her a cigarette. She took it and he lit her up, still talking. He jerked his thumb back at me. She moved slightly to get a better view, shrugged and nodded. Tommy crooked a finger at me.

I went up the path and Tommy gave me one of his winning smiles, swivelling a little to include the woman in it. 'This is Coralie, Cliff, my man. Says you have to excuse the mess in the house.'

I nodded. The toddler scuttled away and the infant on Coralie's hip sucked on its dummy. Coralie was in her twenties, pale and freckled with greasy, mousy-blonde hair. Her heavy breasts had leaked, leaving stains on her faded Panthers sweatshirt. The finger she used to flick her hair away from her eyes was heavily nicotine-stained, but she blew smoke away from the baby. She pressed herself against the doorway to let me through. The smell hit me like a grenade—fried food, sweat, tobacco smoke and despair.

Coralie pushed past me on her way to the back of the place. 'That fuckin' money's in my hand in ten fuckin' minutes, Tommy, or I'm putting the men on you.'

'No worries,' Tommy said. 'Make it snappy, Cliff.'

I was more than willing. Lou had said she talked to Billie in the front bedroom to the right of the passage. I went there and found it contained a double bed, a built-in wardrobe and a chest of drawers. The room was like an op-shop sorting area with clothes and bedding and plastic bags strewn about. I pushed through the detritus and slid open the middle drawer in the chest. It came easily and I emptied the contents on the bed and turned it over. A polaroid photograph was cellotaped to the underside and I eased it free.

'Hey,' Tommy said. 'That's worth a bonus. How about the fifty?'

After a quick look at it, I put the photograph in my shirt pocket. I picked the stuff up and restored it to the drawer. Slid it home. I gave Tommy his fifty.

'How long's she been here?'

He shrugged. 'Coupla weeks.'

'How many kids has she got?'

'Four.'

'No bloke?'

He shook his head.

'Get her back.'

He went down the hall and after a few minutes returned with Coralie, minus baby, in tow, both of them with fresh cigarettes going.

'Thanks,' I said. I gave her four fifties, making sure Tommy saw them. 'Good luck.'

Her dull, defeated eyes barely blinked as she took the money. She stood crookedly, as if perpetually ready to carry a child on her hip.

'You said a hundred,' Tommy complained as we reached the car.

'She needed it. Let's see if you can deliver.'

'Best to get away from here, brother. When I said no bloke, they come and go, like.'

We drove off and Tommy asked to go back to the shopping centre. 'I'm hungry, man. Wanna get something to eat.'

'Get me a coffee, then.'

I sat on a seat near the car park. If he'd been bluffing about knowing Billie I wouldn't see him again. If he was stalling, working up a story, it might take a while. The day was getting hot and there were fewer people around. The health centre looked to have closed and the homeboys had drifted off somewhere. Tommy came back with a packet of chicken and chips, a bottle of coke and a coffee in a styrofoam cup. He put the lot down and sank onto the seat with a sigh. He reached into a pocket and brought out a stirring stick and several packets of sugar. He tore open his package, ripped off a piece of chicken and stuffed it into his mouth with a fistful of chips. He chewed no more than he needed to, swallowed and sighed again. He was hungry all right.

The coffee was thin so I put in sugar to give it some taste. He ate some more and drank his coke. I took the photo from my pocket and showed it to him. Billie fitted Lou's description pretty well—blonde, good looking, a bit tough but with a good smile and lively eyes. She wore a tight top and even tighter pants. Heels. She was smiling down at the dark-skinned boy as if he was the most precious thing on earth. Tommy looked at the photo, still chewing, but more slowly.

'Yeah, that's her.'

'What about the kid?'

'How old's this picture?'

'I've been told it could be five years.'

'So the kid's grown and that. I dunno, he might be around.'

'Is *she* around?'

Now he was definitely stalling. He took a long swig on his coke and reached for his cigarettes. I stopped him.

'C'mon, Tommy. If you want the money . . .'

'Money ain't everything.'

'True.'

'But if you got none, nothin' ain't nothin'.'

'If I want philosophy I can read a book.'

'We've gotta problem.'

'We?'

'You 'cos you want the woman and me 'cos I want the dough.'

'Look, it's hot. I got bashed the other night and I'm hurting a bit. You've earned your fifty but there's not a bloody cent more unless you tell me what you know. Up to you. It's nothing to me, the money—just an expense for my client.'

'Good game you're in, brother.'

I took off my sunglasses and showed him the battered eye. 'You reckon?'

'Shit. You gotta gun, Cliff?'

Because of what I'd heard about Liston and Billie and what I knew about Eddie Flannery, I had my Smith & Wesson in the glove box, but I wasn't about to tell that to Tommy.

'I might have,' I said.

'You better. You heard Coralie say something about putting the men onto me if I fucked her over?'

I nodded.

'She's talkin' about some people who sort of run things around here. Mostly coconuts, but with some Kooris and gubbahs thrown in, like.'

'Yes?'

'They handle the evictions and that for the Department. Booted my dad out a while ago and he's gone back to the Block. I'm still hangin' here trying to get a job.'

'The woman?'

'I seen her with one of them. Real tough bastard named Yoli. Lives here, but I dunno if she's still around.'

'When did you last see her?'

'Coupla days ago. Couldn't miss her though with the fair hair. Not usual around here. She looked crook. And I heard Yoli call her Billie—well, he like shouted at her to go inside. Heard you say the name when you was talking to Big Johnny.'

'Another hundred if you show me where he lives.'

He shook his head. 'Two hundred, man. I'll have to get the fuck outa here. If Yoli found out I told you he'd fuckin' kill me.'

'All right. Yoli, is that a nickname? What's his full name?'

'Yolande something—Potare, Potato, the funny names they got, the fuckin' Fijis. I can give you the address but I can't go with you, understand?'

I took out my wallet and gave him two fifties. 'That's for the address. I'll meet you later anywhere you say to give you the rest.'

'Fuck, you mightn't show.'

'So we're both taking a chance.'

'How long're you goin' to be?'

'I don't know.'

He gave me the address and said he'd wait for me at the Campbelltown railway station for the rest of the afternoon. He gathered up the remainder of his food and dropped it with the coke bottle into the nearest bin. He gave me a good citizen grin, lit a cigarette and walked away.

7

The address Tommy gave me was the end unit in a row a few streets back from the shopping centre. The units were all of a piece—two storeyed but narrow with minimal front yards and not much more space at the back. The one I was interested in at least had some grass and a few shrubs at the side. I drove past it twice, the second time more quickly. It wasn't smarter or shabbier than the others, although the car parked outside looked to be derelict or close to it and there was a non-operational washing machine sitting out in the sun in the side yard.

I parked in the thin shade thrown by a struggling tree at the edge of the recreation area and thought the matter over. Yoli sounded like a handful and I was in no condition to go up against an aggressive Polynesian vigilante who no doubt had plenty of backup.

The people had thinned out before, presumably going home for lunch. Now the public space was filling up again, with kids kicking a soccer ball around, shoppers carrying plastic bags from the supermarket and others gathering for a meeting of some kind at the primary school. A couple of 180-centimetre plus teenage boys whizzed around on bikes so small their knees were up under their chins as they pedalled. One of them could've been Billie's boy.

I drove back to the street and parked where I could keep the unit in sight and not be seen myself. There were several cars parked nearby, more than was common in the area. The police car cruised up and parked in front of me. One of the cops got busy checking on my registration; the other got out and walked back towards me.

'Could I see your licence, sir?'

I handed it to him and he went back to the car and conferred with his colleague. He was young, unimpressed by the Falcon, unimpressed by me. I got out and stood by the car so I wouldn't be peering up at him. He handed back the licence.

'Spotted you around over the past hour and a bit, Mr Hardy. Would you tell me what you're doing here?'

I took out the folder with my PEA licence and showed it to him. 'I'm working.'

'Doing what?'

I shook my head. 'I'm not causing any trouble.'

'You better not. If you're still here when we come around again we'll cause some trouble for you.'

Fair enough. The fight outside the protection centre, the shutdown bottle shop and the graffiti suggested that the area was volatile with its racial mixture and poverty. They didn't need the likes of me. He hitched the belt holding all the equipment they carry these days, went back to his car and they drove off.

I still had no idea what to do and now I was under time pressure. A minute later a car pulled up outside the unit. The man who got out made the Hilux 4WD look small—John Manuma. Seeing him at full stretch for the second time, I realised he was as big a man as I'd ever seen anywhere. It made me even more reluctant to tackle the place.

Manuma stepped over the gate, marched up to the front door and went straight in. He stayed for less than five minutes, stalked back to his car looking angry, and drove away. Could he be an ally despite our earlier encounter? I doubted it. Then she came out. Billie. Had to be. She had the platinum hair, the short skirt and skimpy top, the legs, the stacked-heel sandals. She shouted something back at the door of the unit as it was slammed shut, then she spun around and went towards her car. With a snarl on her face and her shoulders thrown aggressively back, she reminded me of Mike Carlton's description of Rose Hancock—all tits and teeth.

Her car was a white VW Golf. She slung her shoulder bag inside, got in, gunned the motor and took off, burning rubber. I was glad to be up and running after all the indecision. I let her get well ahead and followed, feeling guilty about being relieved I hadn't had to front the vigilantes, but confident, at last, of making some progress. She kept up a steady speed just above the limit, looking as keen to leave Liston behind her as I was. She slowed down through Campbelltown, observed the signs and the limits, and was easy to follow. I spared a brief thought for Tommy as I passed the railway station but nothing more. He'd done okay and, as it turned out, I hadn't put him in jeopardy.

The Golf picked up speed. Not Billie's kind of car, I would have thought, but she drove it well, asserting herself but not dangerously. For no good reason other than what I'd been told about Billie, I expected her to take the highway to the big smoke. Not so. She headed down the road to everywhere south of Sydney and I settled back for a long drive. Fooled me again. We reached the old town of Picton. It's funny the things that come back to you. I remember having to do a school project on country towns and Picton was one that fell to me. All I remember is that it was named after a general who got killed at the Battle of Waterloo. At that age I was more interested in battles than economics, still am for that matter. So I don't remember what got Picton established. Mining probably, and dairying—always safe bets.

She pulled in at a pub. Thank you, Billie, I thought. Thank you very much.

She got out, hoisted her bag onto her shoulder, and went into the pub. It was old style with a balcony running around the front and sides one floor up and other remnants of the original structure not ruined by probably several phases of renovation. It looked welcoming. I followed her into the bar and saw her heading off to the women's toilet. Maybe she was just paying a visit for that purpose. I hoped not. I ordered a light beer and was relieved when she came out, ordered a gin and tonic and took the drink through to an outside area where she could smoke. She lit up and settled down at a table with a view across some paddocks to the hills.

My eye was throbbing. I swallowed a couple of painkillers with the last of the middy and ordered another. I bought a packet of chips at the machine and munched them slowly, trying not to be too obvious about watching the woman. Five or six people were in the bar minding their own business. A television set was tuned to the races and I looked up at it from time to time, pretending an interest. With my glass half empty I ordered a gin and tonic, surprising the barman.

'For the lady,' I said, pointing.

He nodded, more interested in the races.

I had another good, long look at her as he prepared the drinks. Tommy had said she'd looked ill when he'd seen her. Must have made a quick recovery because she looked healthy now. Back straight, head up. What she really looked was angry. She flicked ash from her cigarette without caring where it went and sipped her drink without apparent pleasure.

'Shit,' the barman said, and I gathered his horse had lost as they mostly do.

I took the drinks through to the outside sitting area and reached over her shoulder to put the gin down in front of her.

'Hello, Billie,' I said.

I moved around to face her and she looked at me as if I'd just tipped the drink down the front of her top.

'My name's not Billie,' she said. 'And who the hell are you?'

8

It took us quite a while and another drink to get it sorted out. Her name was Sharon Marchant, and she was Billie's younger sister.

'I know we look alike,' she said after a few preliminary exchanges, 'but we're not twins. I'm taller; she's thinner.'

'I've only seen a photo that goes back a few years.'

I said I'd followed her from Liston, showed her my credentials and gave her a carefully constructed version of the reason for my interest in her sister. I implied that money could be a factor, but didn't say how much or how it might be earned. She listened, smoking, drinking. Then I asked the obvious question.

'So what were you doing in Liston, Sharon?'

She wasn't about to jump into anything. 'Have you got the number for this client of yours?'

'Sure.'

She took a mobile phone from her bag and raised an eyebrow. I read off the number from Lou's card and she dialled it.

'Hello, Ms Kramer? My name is Sharon Marchant. I'm Billie's sister. I understand you talked to her not so long ago—that right?'

There aren't many things worse than being excluded from a conversation that interests you intensely. I fiddled with my glass.

'Okay. And you've hired a man named Cliff Hardy to help you?'

The painkillers and the alcohol had cut in. I was feeling competent, in control, and let my gaze wander to the horizon. Maybe the painkillers were having a mind-altering effect because I was suddenly aware of what had been nagging at me since I'd reached Campbelltown. The sky was immense, the horizon far distant and human problems seemed less important than they do in the enclosed environments of the city. Careful, Cliff, I thought, you've got a living to earn.

Sharon closed her phone and picked up her glass. 'She wanted to talk to you but I said she could do it on her own dime.'

'My mobile's in the car. I kind of dislike it.'

She shrugged.

I guessed her age at around forty but she was carrying it well. Her figure was firm and her face, though lined, was still taut where it mattered. Those Marchant genes had to be good. 'Well, I'll tell you why I was in that shithole. Billie's there. She's shacked up with this Tongan arsehole, Yolande.'

'I've heard of him. Some kind of vigilante?'

'I dunno about that. He's a God botherer, like a lot of them, and he's trying to get her off stuff.'

'Stuff?'

She raised her glass and took a pull on the cigarette she'd puffed on throughout the phone call. 'Fags and booze, speed—you name it. She got desperate and called me and I went there. Shit!'

She ground out the cigarette. 'They're praying over her when she's asleep and reading the Bible at her and singing their hymns and it's driving her crazy. I tried to get her to come away with me and I reckon she was almost ready to even though she's in a mind-fucked fog, and then that big bastard arrived.'

'Manuma.'

'Right. He's got them all under the thumb. Shit, I don't know what to do. She's my sister and I love her, but . . . I know she's trouble. Fair killed our mum.'

'What about the boy?'

She almost dropped her lighter on its way to the cigarette in her mouth. 'You know about him?'

I showed her the photograph.

She got the cigarette lit, inexpertly. 'How did you get this?'

I told her. It seemed to make her take my presence and interest in her sister more seriously. She flattened out a corner of the photo that had got bent. 'She'd love to have this back, I'm sure.'

'Why would she leave it behind?'

'She overdosed accidentally on some bad shit. Yolande packed her up and moved her to his place. She's been there ever since, under . . . what d'you call it? House arrest. Getting the Jesus treatment. What she needs is proper stuff—detoxification, counselling and that.'

'Is this Yolande the boy's father? What's his name by the way?'

'Samuel. Sam. No, not Yolande. That's only been going on for a couple of years. Sam came along, oh, fifteen years ago.'

'Before Eddie?'

She blew smoke. 'You do know a bit, don't you?'

'I knew Eddie. He was in the same game, but he played by different rules.'

'Eddie,' she said. 'What a loser. To tell you the truth, I don't think Billie knows who Sam's father was. She had a thing for black blokes at the time.'

'Black as in?'

She shrugged. 'Kooris, mostly. We both went that way for a while. We're said to have a touch of it ourselves, would you believe?'

'Plenty do, they say. A lot more than know it or admit it. But you've dodged the question. Where's Sam now?'

All of a sudden, the initial wariness she'd displayed was back. 'Look, you've bought me a couple of drinks and showed you're caught up in something involving Billie. But I don't know anything about this Clement you mentioned. Why d'you want to know about Sam?'

I took off the sunglasses and let her see my eye. 'My client, Lou Kramer, the woman you just spoke to, claims that Clement had Eddie Flannery killed because he knew something about Clement's business and tried to make a quid out of it. Clement found out I was working for Lou and I copped this for my trouble. Lou thinks Billie might know what Eddie knew and, if she does, she's in danger. The kid makes her vulnerable if Clement gets wind of him. Does any of this make sense?'

'I need another drink.'

'You'll be too high to drive.'

'I can walk. I live here. Get me a drink while I think this over a bit.'

I kept my eye on her while I got the drink, wondering whether she might do a runner. But she sat, apparently doing what she said—thinking. I glanced out of the window at my car and thought Lou Kramer must be frantically trying to call me on the mobile. Given the way she'd been playing things I didn't mind the ball being in my court for a bit. I put the drink down on a coaster near the ashtray.

'Not having one?'

'I'll be driving.'

'You're going to have to tell me a bit more about this woman you're working for.'

I'd been very sketchy on that and a few other matters and now I filled in some details.

'How much money's she making out of this?'

'I don't know, but a good deal. Clement's a high profile figure, a big poppy. When they come down there's always a lot of interest. Plus he's got connections to other people who're even more interesting than him.'

'Like?'

If I mentioned Peter Scriven and the lost millions she'd know who I was talking about—every news magazine in the country had run articles on him and his face was as familiar as Ian Thorpe's. But I wasn't quite ready to go that far, talking that kind of money, which, anyway, Lou had said wasn't her main interest. I pushed some chip fragments around the wet table top.

'Look, Sharon, we're fencing here. You're playing Sam's whereabouts close to your chest and I'm inclined to do the same from my end. How about you tell me a bit about yourself, your connection with Billie and Sam and Eddie, and we can take it from there.'

She was half drunk by now. 'You're a careful type, aren't you?'

'Middle name.'

She sighed and suddenly looked tired and every day of her age. She fiddled with an unlit cigarette and went into a rambling account of her life, almost from day one to now. Connected narrative wasn't her strong suit and the grog wasn't helping. She and Billie were only two years apart and they'd been very close as kids. Both tearaways, drop-outs, broken home products. In her twenties Sharon had slowed down, married but it didn't last, had a child, gone to art school and now earned her living as a children's book illustrator and giving painting lessons. Billie had stayed on her original track with Sam being about the only good thing that had happened to her.

'Certainly couldn't call Eddie that,' she said, 'or Yoli. I got Sam away from Billie a few years ago. I know where he is, she doesn't.'

'What about your child?'

'She's fine. I was lucky. Her dad's supportive, sort of. She's in her first year at uni. Flats in Campbelltown, comes home a lot.' She raised her glass, snapped the cigarette in half with her other hand and dropped the pieces into the ashtray. 'You probably won't believe me, but this is the most serious drinking and smoking I've done in years.'

She hitched at the neck of her top. 'And I don't normally dress like this. I'm usually in pants and T-shirts, and Billie can't stand to see it. She reckons I'm just proving I've got some qualifications and a real job and that all she's ever been any good at was screwing. So I bought the fags and tarted up, went blonde again even, to try to get her approval and get her away from that place. Didn't work.'

I was finding her impressive and credible, but that alone put me on the defensive. I couldn't count the number of times people, women in particular, had presented one face to me only for me to find that they had quite another. And she'd presented two quite convincing faces already.

'Look, Sharon, why don't I drive you home and you can get some coffee inside you and straighten up. I'll call my client and talk a few things over with her. I think there's a way forward from all this.'

She nodded and looped her bag onto her shoulder. 'And you'll want to see some of the books so you can see I'm not lying.'

I grinned at her. 'Wouldn't hurt.'

'Suspicious bastard.'

I reached for the cigarettes.

'Leave 'em,' she said.

Sharon went to her car and retrieved a few folders and a cloth bag, locked the Golf and got into my Falcon.

'Don't spend up big on maintenance, do you?'

'It's what's under the bonnet that matters. You wash 'em, they just get dirty again.'

We buckled up. 'Where to?' I said.

'Keep going and I'll tell you. I'm out of town a bit, in the hills.'

A bit turned out to be the best part of ten kilometres with a good deal of it on a narrow, climbing, twisting dirt road. I wouldn't have fancied her chances of staying on it unless she could carry her liquor a lot better than it seemed. The hill country had a soothing effect on her and she gradually looked more comfortable, less strained. I'm a coast man myself, trees don't do a lot for me unless they're Norfolk Island pines fringing a beach, but I had to admit the quiet had an appeal. I wound down the window a bit further and sniffed the scents of an Australian bush summer in the making.

As if she was reading my mind she said, still slurring a little, 'Where d' you live?'

'Glebe.'

'Jesus, I lived there a while back. Couldn't hack the pace and the stink now.'

'Where did you grow up?'

'Liverpool—worse.'

'I spent some time there when I worked for an insurance company.'

'Your lungs must be lead coated. Righto, round here and you'll see a track leading off to the right. Careful now, it's narrow and there's a sort of ditch you have to creep over.'

I slowed down and made the turn. The ditch gave my suspension a workout and then we were climbing steadily again with the trees and scrub close on both sides, almost brushing the car.

'I found this old miner's shack a few years ago. I'm leasing it now but hoping to—Oh, Jesus!'

The shack was in view in the middle of a small clearing, but so was a 4WD, parked right by the dwelling. Massive John Manuma was standing with his back to the car and arms folded, looking straight at us.

9

I hit the brake hard. 'What the hell does he want?'

Sharon had sobered at the sight of him. 'The same as you—Sam, to put pressure on Billie.'

Manuma must have recognised my car because he came forward, bent to pick up a solid bit of tree branch and snapped it to a handy length over his knee.

'Oh, God,' Sharon said. 'Back up! Go!'

'No chance.' The track was narrow and trees grew close in on both sides. There was enough space, just, but not the time to do a three-point turn and I didn't fancy reversing at pace on the loose dirt. I left the car in neutral with the motor running, reached into the glove box and unshipped the .38.

'What're you doing?'

'Sit still. It'll be all right.'

I got out and let Manuma see the gun. He was about twenty metres away, swinging his waddy. I raised the gun and sighted on his huge chest.

'Stop there!'

He did, but he was poised to come on. 'You won't shoot me.'

I lowered my aim. 'I won't shoot you in the chest, you're right. But I'll put a couple in your legs and what if I miss, go a bit high? I mean it . . . Johnny. Put down the fucking stick, take out your car keys and drop them on the ground or I swear I'll cripple you. I've done it before.'

'I just want to talk to her.'

'Sure you do. Well, we might arrange that, but not here, not now.' I moved the pistol a fraction. 'Do it . . . Johnny.'

He hated me addressing him that way, but he reached into his pants pocket, took out the keys and dropped them without taking his eyes off me. This guy had been in tight situations before and knew how to behave. Me too, but his size and composure were impressive and I knew I couldn't control him without shooting for much longer. Praying she could drive a manual, I gestured at Sharon to turn the Falcon around: my waving fingers said do it slowly.

'Big mistake, you making.'

'Shut up!'

I heard the wheels on the dirt, a slight bump, the grind of gears, and then two sharp beeps on the horn.

I backed a few steps and saw he was preparing to rush me.

'I'm good with this at thirty metres,' I said, 'bit erratic after that. I'd advise you to keep your distance.'

I retreated. Give him his due, he came after me, closing a little, probably hoping I'd trip over. I didn't. I reached the car, got in and Sharon gave it the gas, slewing back down the track.

'D'you think he'll follow us?' she said as she got the car under full control and slowed down a touch.

'Would in an American movie.'

She giggled. 'I hate to admit it, but that was sort of exciting. Would you really have shot him?'

'I don't know.'

'You want to drive?'

'No, you're doing fine.' I looked back when we hit a straight stretch but there was no sign of pursuit. 'I took a punt you'd be able to drive a manual.'

'Are you kidding? We started off in old bomb Holdens and Vdubs. I still like the Vdubs.'

'Yeah, they're good.' I realised I'd kept the pistol in my hand and shoved it back in the glove box.

'How many people have you shot, Cliff?'

'Not many lately and I'm not anxious to add to the tally. The paperwork's horrendous.'

'You're trying to impress me with your toughness.'

'Right. And myself.'

We drove on in silence for a while and reached the main road. She made the turn and pulled over. 'Now what?' she said.

'My guess is he'll hang around and then probably send someone to keep an eye on the place. You can't go back for a bit.'

'Great. I've got a living to earn. I've got jobs on hand and a class on Tuesday.'

'Well, that gives us a couple of days. I think you ought to meet up with Lou Kramer and talk a few things through.'

'Like where Sam is?'

'And money to help Billie.'

'Shove over.' She got out and went around to the passenger side. I slid across as she got in, scrabbling in her shoulder bag. She pulled out her wallet.

'I've got twenty-three dollars in cash and about another sixty in my keycard account. That's it. My Mastercard's at its limit. How'm I going to get by? I've got no clothes . . . no . . .'

The adrenalin fuelling her through the confrontation with Manuma and the helter-skelter drive had ebbed away. She let her head drop back and her body sag.

I reached over and put my hand gently on her shoulder. 'You can stay at my place. Lou Kramer's pretty much your size. I'll ask her to bring some clothes. And you can phone your kid and tell her what you need to.'

'Okay,' she said. 'Okay. You win.'

But it didn't feel anything like a win. Not yet, not by a long stretch.

I took it easy on the drive back to Sydney to give Sharon time to adjust to what was happening. She looked disconsolate for a while but brightened up when we got closer in.

'I used to love this place,' she said, 'the people, the energy, the pubs . . .'

'I still do.'

'It's different for men. When a woman reaches a certain age . . .'

'Come on, that's old-style thinking. Anyway, the thing about Sydney is you can be what you want to be. Young and sensible, old and silly—you'll find somewhere it's acceptable.'

'You really believe that?'

'I do.'

'First I've heard of it. Well, I prefer the country now—the quiet, the routines, the trees and everything.'

I nodded and kept driving. She was well on the way to being her balanced self and she was going to need to be to cope with what was coming. The painkillers had worn off and I was feeling the odd stab around the eye. I must've reacted.

'What's wrong?'

'Bloody eye hurts a bit still.'

'Did this Clement do that?'

'Not him. One of his helpers.'

'And you'd like to meet up with him again?'

'Under the right circumstances.'

'What would they be?'

'When the eye doesn't hurt. But the point is there's something big at stake here. I don't know what it is, but Lou Kramer and Billie and Sam and me and now you, possibly, are all caught up in it.'

'I've been doing some thinking. Maybe Billie's safest where she is with the Bible-bashers, and Sam the same.'

'Maybe. But d'you think cold turkey and Jesus are really going to work with Billie?'

'No, but it could be a toss-up between that and millionaires who have thugs to bash people.'

'Hmm. Let's at least hear what Lou Kramer has to say. Here's Glebe Point Road. Almost home.'

I drove past my house a couple of times, checking the street for anything out of the ordinary. Sharon looked puzzled.

'What're you doing?'

'Just being careful.'

A while ago I installed an alarm, and security doors front and back and on the windows. Hated to do it and resented the expense, but a break-in and a nasty encounter with an aggrieved client had made it necessary. I did the unlocking and deactivated the alarm.

Sharon took a look at the two rooms off the passage, glanced up the stairs with its faded runner and two uprights missing on the rail, and went through to the kitchen—renovated in the sixties, but not since.

'Good place,' she said. 'Worth a bit.'

'Bought for a song when Glebe was still Glebe. Have a seat. D'you want coffee or a drink?'

'I want a sleep.'

'Upstairs, at the back. Titchy bathroom next door. Should be a towel in it. I mostly use the one down here.'

She smiled. 'Titchy?'

'When I was young, little things were called titchy. Small blokes were always Titch.'

'You probably talked about bodgies and widgies.'

'That was more a Melbourne thing, I think.' I got her a glass of water and a couple of painkillers. 'These're for the head. Get it down and then we'll have a talk before I contact Lou.'

She nodded and went up the stairs, dragging her feet. I heard the shower running and then the spare room door close. Cliff the Good Samaritan needed some more Panadeine Forte and a drink.

I did my thing with the names and the circles and squares and connecting arrows and dotted lines in my notebook, while I washed down the tablets with a big glass of cask red. The day had given me quite a few more entries to make. I put a big question mark alongside my note on Mr X and his Beemer's registration number and knew that there at least I was on track to learn something. The day cooled down the way it does at this time of year; I found a clean flannel shirt and hung it on the knob of the spare room door.

'No, no, no.'

She was moaning in her sleep. Sharon was obviously in better mental and physical condition than her sister, but we all have our demons. I left my mobile switched off and in the car. I'd talk to Lou Kramer when Sharon and I were ready. I was awaiting the bank notice about the dishonoured cheque. Bound to come. Re-present and wait how long? I wasn't prepared to give my client quite everything I knew or suspected just yet. As I'd said to Sharon—call me careful.

I went out to the car and retrieved my mobile and the pistol. I was about to turn the mobile on when the phone in the house rang. The machine picked up.

'Hardy, where the hell are you? What's going on? I—'

I grabbed the phone. 'Take it easy, Lou. I'm here. Everything's more or less under control.'

'Says you. That woman who rang me. What're you playing at? I've been trying your mobile for hours ever since.'

'As she told you, she's Billie Marchant's sister. Hang on.'

I went to the stairs and listened but heard nothing.

'What now?' Lou snapped when I got back on the line.

'I've got her with me here. We've had developments. I found Billie.'

'Great. Where is she?'

'Still where I found her. Listen, Lou, it's all a bit tricky. But the sister knows where Billie's son is and she's halfway to helping us get hold of Billie. So calm down.'

'All right, all right. But you know how important talking to Billie is to me.'

Me, me, me, I thought. I said, 'To you, yeah. But Billie's strung out and with some dangerous and strange people and there's the kid's safety to consider.'

I could sense her fighting for control, trying to keep the aggression and impatience out of her tone. 'You're calling the shots,' she said.

'Sort of. I want you to come to my place tonight and talk things over with Sharon. She's about your size and she needs some clothes, something functional—jeans, a blouse, a jacket, sandals, like that.'

Lou laughed. 'She's naked? Hardy, you devil.'

I let her have that one. 'And some money.'

'Shit. How much?'

'Say a hundred bucks.'

'All right, you had me worried for a minute.'

'The subject'll come up again, I guarantee. And one more thing, Lou—don't tell anyone about this, and I mean anyone. Okay?'

'Sure, but how about you give her the hundred and put it on your account. I don't think you've knocked down that retainer yet.'

'The cheque hasn't been honoured yet.'

'It will be. What's the address and what time do you want me there?'

I looked at my watch. 'About seven. We'll be having a curry. D'you like curry?'

'No,' she said and hung up.

Despite myself, the election talk was sucking me in. The opposition was promising free health care for citizens over seventy-five. Not yet. The government wanted to make it easier for small business to sack people and was swearing to keep interest rates low. No appeal for me there. If small business had its way they'd be putting people on and laying them off as it suited them, and devil take the hindmost. And I didn't have a mortgage any longer.

A while back I'd helped a lawyer who was trying to get a refugee out of a detention centre. Didn't happen. The detention centres hadn't rated a mention so far to my knowledge. I couldn't think of a single reason to vote for either of the major parties. The Greens in the Senate, maybe, to keep the bastards honest, the way the Democrats hadn't.

10

Sharon got up and heard me working on the computer in the room next to where she'd slept. She came in wearing my flannie.

'What're you doing?'

'Just seeing what I can find on Clement.'

'Much?'

'Too much and probably all bullshit. I looked up that community protection mob as well. All very churchy, but there was a bloke mentioned as a counsellor that I've heard of, a Maori.'

'And?'

'Used to be standover man working for a fight promoter.'

'He probably got born again.'

'Yeah, in his case it wouldn't hurt. How're you feeling?'

She fingered the shirt which came down to her knees. 'This's more like me. Wouldn't go with the sandals though.'

I told her Lou Kramer was coming over with some clothes and to have a talk.

'You said we could discuss that first.'

'I know. Sorry. She called and there wasn't any other way to handle it.'

She wasn't happy but she let it go. She called her daughter and told her she was in the city for a day or two with a friend. She grinned as she listened.

'Behave yourself. Listen, darling, my car's parked at the pub. Could you get Craig to run you out there and pick it up? You've got a key. You could hang on to it for me for a couple of days . . . In your dreams. Thanks, love. Bye.'

She hung up. The conversation had improved her mood. 'She worries about my love life, or lack of one.'

'Sounds as if you get along well.'

'We do.' I'd taken another glass of red up to the computer with me and she looked at it. 'I could go some of that now.'

'Do you like curry?'

'Love it. Take out, right? I looked around your kitchen and didn't see any cumin and coriander.'

'That's right. When I curry something, mostly sausages, I do it with the help of Clive of India.'

'Yuk. Well, if you had the fixings I'd offer to make it, but you don't and I don't reckon I'm quite up to cooking just now. I can, though.'

'That's okay. You've had a hard day and there's a very good place up the street.'

I went out on foot to the Taste of India. A little light rain had fallen, laying the dust and setting free the scents from the gardens. When I first got to Glebe the small spaces in front of most of the terraces were filled with weeds, rubbish, and supermarket trolleys. Now they sprouted well-tended native gardens, and the old, rusted, gap-toothed wrought iron fences had been replaced by intact modern versions of the same thing. The security doors and window bars were another innovation.

We had the food spread out in its containers on the eating bench in the kitchen by seven o'clock. We were both hungry and got straight into it. We ate and drank in silence for a while.

'No woman, Cliff?' Sharon said as she took a pause.

'Not as of now.'

'Why's that?'

'They don't stick around, or I don't, or both.'

'Can't commit?'

I forked in some rogan josh and chewed on it. 'Maybe,' I said, 'but it's more than that. It's to do with the work. If you'd lived in Canberra, say, that's where I'd be tonight. Anyone living with me'd be on their own a good bit of the time. Hard to plan a night out.'

'Let alone a family.'

'Let alone.'

'So, no kids?'

'I've got a daughter I didn't know about until she was grown up. For one reason or another her mother didn't let on to me. I see her from time to time now but that's about it. I'm glad she's there and doing okay, but I can't claim any credit for it.'

'I can claim it for mine.'

'You're lucky.'

She ate a few mouthfuls, then shook her head. 'Has to be more to it than that. These days there's lots of professional women leading busy lives, working odd hours. They don't require their blokes to be home by six for tea. And there's more to you than you say. I've had a look at your books.'

'I suppose so. But when I'm working, and that's pretty much all the time to make a living, I get very preoccupied. Nothing much left over.'

'Are you happy about it?'

Before I could answer the doorbell rang.

'That'll be Lou.'

'What's she like?'

'Tricky.'

Lou trooped in wearing jeans, a white T-shirt and a denim jacket. She carried an overnight bag, her backpack and a bottle of white wine. I introduced the two and Lou handed over the bag. 'Some clothes as requested. Hope they're your size.'

'Thanks,' Sharon said, 'I'll get them back to you soon as.'

'I can make you a sandwich, Lou.'

She shook her head and smiled. 'I was just pissed off with you. I like curry. Got enough?'

We finished the food down to the last grain of rice and scrap of pappadum. Sharon had had a glass of red and accepted a small one of Lou's white. I poured myself a bigger one. Lou said she'd wait for coffee. 'I've still got work to do tonight. Can we get down to it?'

We sat around the low table in the living room and I ran quickly through the events of the day. The two women eyed each other off in a way that didn't fill me with optimism. A mutual dislike was immediately apparent.

'My sister's in a very bad way,' Sharon said. 'I reckon her physical and mental health are in danger and I'd like to get her away.'

'Understood,' Lou said, 'and you think your knowing where the kid is gives you some leverage.'

'I wouldn't put it quite like that.'

'How would you . . . never mind. Why can't we just get some sort of court order? Have the cops take her away?'

'I don't think it'd be quite that easy, Lou,' I said. 'You'd have to give some sort of notice of the proceedings and the people she's with would probably just move her. From what I can gather there's a sort of vigilante network out there. They'd probably know as soon as some outside cops or social workers got anywhere near the place.'

Lou drank her coffee in a couple of gulps and I topped her up. 'Okay,' she said. 'You mentioned money on the phone, Cliff. What's on your mind?'

'If we can get Billie away there's going to have to be money to take care of her—doctors, detox, rehab—all that.'

'How much?'

Sharon almost snapped to attention. 'I know what's on your mind, Ms Kramer. You're thinking I'm in this to do myself some good.'

Lou shrugged. 'You said it, not me.'

'Shit,' Sharon said. She went out to the kitchen and I heard the cork coming out of the bottle.

'Flaky, like her sister,' Lou murmured.

'Take it easy. She's your only avenue to Billie.'

Sharon came back in and stood behind her chair. 'I don't know about this, Cliff.'

'I was hasty,' Lou said. 'I'm sure I can organise some money. Would twenty thousand do it?'

I tried not to react too obviously. I had no idea how much Lou's advance had been, but the fact that she was still working at the paper suggested it wasn't a lot. How would she lay her hands on twenty grand? The only answer I could think of was Mr X, and that gave me something else to worry about.

Lou had turned on the charm as she spoke, something some people can do at will. She smiled, repeated her apology to Sharon and sucked her in, at least for the moment.

Sharon said, 'That amount would probably do, but I still don't know how to get Billie away. I mean, if there was some way I could tell her about the help we can offer and that she could see Sam, she'd probably cooperate. But how?'

They both looked at me. Luckily, I thought I had an answer but I wasn't going to tell them, particularly Lou, just yet. 'There could be a way. I'll have to work on it.'

Lou tried to grill Sharon about Billie's state of mind—her memory, her grasp on reality—but Sharon wasn't forthcoming. Eventually Lou gave up. 'Keep me informed, Cliff. A bit better than you have so far, if I may say so. And I'll see what I can do about the money.' She gave Sharon a nod and I showed her to the door.

'Don't get distracted,' she said as she walked out. I stood at the gate and watched her until she was safely in her car and driving away. All part of the service.

Sharon was quietly swearing. 'I wish I hadn't had those cigarettes. I gave them up years ago and that burst has brought the craving back. Haven't got any, have you?'

'No. I could go out.'

She shook her head. 'No, just have to see it through. I didn't care for your client.'

I started to clean up the mugs and glasses. 'I noticed.'

'She's not the kind of woman other women trust.'

'I'm with the other women.'

'You don't trust her?'

'No. For one thing, probably minor, her retainer cheque didn't clear. And she's holding things back.'

'What things?'

'I don't know. People who hire private detectives think they have a problem. Usually they have a couple of problems, sometimes ones they don't know about.'

She thought that over as she drank the last of her wine. 'You ought to write a book on it.'

'No way.'

She yawned. 'I'm tired even after that kip. Probably the wine. Hey, the curry was good.'

She helped me clean up and stack the dishwasher, not that there was much to stack. Lou's bottle went into the milk crate that forms the halfway house to the recycling bin. I jiggled the cask. 'We hammered the red a bit.'

'Yeah. Well . . .'

It was one of those moments that could've led to something intimate, but we both realised it wasn't the time. I jumped in with practical points.

'Before you go up, is there a neighbour anywhere near your place up there in the sticks?'

'Yes. Why?'

'It'd be a good idea to give them a ring in the morning and ask them to keep an eye on the place. You can come up with some story about a nuisance. One of your students or something. Would the neighbour cooperate?'

'She'd love it. D'you think . . . ?'

I was thinking a number of things. Whether Lou, despite my warning, had told Mr X, and whether he had a significant finger in the pie. What Big John Manuma's motives were. But I reached out and gave her a chaste kiss on the cheek.

'No. Just being super cautious. Goodnight, Sharon.'

. . .

It was a comfort to have someone sleeping in the house, even if the person wasn't a lover or even a friend. Back when I had a mortgage to service, I'd tried having tenants to help with the costs. It hadn't worked too well, partly because the first one I had, Hilde Stoner, had been so good the others didn't measure up. Hilde had married a cop named Frank Parker and the two of them were my best friends. I hadn't seen them for a while and promised myself a night out with them when this case was done.

But as I lay in bed I thought that could be a long way off. There were loose ends everywhere and my feeling that Lou Kramer hadn't been anywhere near straight with me had strengthened. I needed that information about her BMW-driving friend. I drifted off to sleep with thoughts of how I used to come awake with the smell of Hilde's coffee wafting up the stairs. Hilde was one of those people who made good coffee, using the same equipment and grounds I did to produce my bitter brews.

11

Sunday, bloody Sunday. I couldn't get in touch with my RTA contact to check on Lou Kramer's mysterious dinner companion and I couldn't act on my idea about springing Billie from the God squad. I went for a long walk around Glebe. Sharon slept late and the door was still closed when I got back with the crappy papers and good croissants. I was sitting in the back yard turning over the pages when she came down. She wore old tracksuit pants and a faded T-shirt.

'Pretty daggy,' she said, fingering the hem of the T-shirt. 'Could she spare 'em?'

'Didn't want you to outshine her. Coffee's hot, croissants are by the microwave.

'Very Glebe.'

She came out with a mug and a croissant on a plate. The sun was well up and it was getting warm in the small space. I bricked it years ago, not well, and weeds spring up in the cracks. Helen Broadway, a girlfriend from the last century, had installed a low maintenance garden and it was holding on pretty well in the face of the water restrictions and my neglect. You can just see glimpses of Blackwattle Bay through the apartment blocks and smell the water when the wind's right. This morning it was, and my patch wasn't a bad place to be.

Sharon turned over a few pages uninterestedly. 'You haven't pressed me about Sam.'

I shrugged. 'No need just yet. I take it you can get in touch with him when and if we have to.'

'Right.'

'He's with good people?'

She filled her mouth with pastry and nodded.

'Kooris?'

Another nod. 'I think that's right about us having a bit of Koori in us. Billie and I aren't blondes, not by a long way, and we darken up good in the summer. There was a photo of Mum's mother hidden away in the house and I found it and asked mum. Grandma Jackson was dark. She had the look. Mum was ashamed of it and Dad was a real racist so it wasn't talked about.'

'So Sam's got it on both sides?'

'Yes. We had a brother, Joe, and he was pretty dark. He got arrested for a minor offence and he hanged himself in the lockup.'

'That says something.'

'I'd like Sam to get a proper education and do something useful in Aboriginal affairs . . . if he was interested.'

It was about the longest and most personal statement she'd made when sober, and it seemed to do her some good. She ate another croissant and used her mobile to check on her daughter and the neighbour. She said yes and no a few times and laughed twice.

'That's fine,' she said as she closed the phone. 'But I have to get back by tomorrow night. I can get a train to Campbelltown and Sarah can pick me up.'

'Should be all right. Check again with the neighbour tomorrow. Lou's authorised me to give you a hundred dollars.'

She raised an eyebrow. 'As much as that?'

'I can up it a bit if you'd like.'

'No, that's fine. Can I use your Mac to check on my email?'

She did that and asked me what I was going to do next.

'I'm a bit stymied,' I said. 'I need to check a rego number with my RTA contact and follow up this idea about getting through to Billie, but I can't do either of them today.'

'Pity Craig's not here.'

'Craig?'

'My daughter Sarah's boyfriend. He could probably hack into the RTA computer. Nothing much he can't do in that line.'

'Handy bloke.'

'In more ways than one. He plays football, swims, troubleshoots for various computer people. He drives a Merc.'

It was getting warmer in the yard and the sun was high and strong. 'Why don't we go to Bondi for a swim?' I said. 'Bet you haven't been there in a while.'

'What? In my bra and knickers?'

'Pick up something down there.'

'You're on.'

We drove to Bondi; Sharon bought a swimsuit and left it on under her clothes. The beach and the car park were busy but I found a spot. We went in a couple of times and we lay on the sand with the other lucky citizens of Sydney.

'You've got a proprietorial look,' Sharon said. 'Raised here, were you?'

I pointed south. 'Maroubra. Spent a bit of time here though. They reckon there's a better city beach in Rio de Janeiro, but this'll do me.'

'Yeah.'

I could see what she meant about her skin. It had that underlying smoky look that would darken quickly in the sun. 'Don't spend much time kicking down doors and shooting people, do you, Cliff?'

'As little as possible.'

She tapped the side of her head, Poirot-style. 'The little grey cells?'

'Not much of that either. More patience and persistence.'

As the sun dropped the day cooled quickly and we decamped and fought the traffic back to Glebe. Sharon prowled around, taking books from the shelves and putting them back. Checking the CD holdings. 'This is getting to me,' she said. 'I want to go home.'

'Give it till tomorrow. Ring your neighbour first thing and your daughter and then you can go.'

'I could go now.'

'You could. Wouldn't if I was you.'

'I suppose you're right. What's on telly?'

She made a big omelette and we ate while watching the news and a few other forgettable programs. She picked out a book—Stephen Scheding's *The National Picture,* his account of trying to locate a lost, and possibly nonexistent, painting of George Robinson and the Tasmanian Aborigines. She read the blurb and looked at me.

'Have you read this?'

'Yeah.'

'Why?'

'It's a detective story, sort of.'

'Bullshit.'

'Sharon, I read to amuse myself and fill in the time. That's all.'

'Fill in the time—that's sad.'

I shook my head. 'Nope. Some of the time's full to overflowing.'

She nodded, touched me on the shoulder, and went up the stairs.

The swim had done me good and the bruise and contusion around my eye were healing up nicely. I hadn't had the company of a woman in a relaxed friendly fashion lately and I'd enjoyed it. For all its uncertainties so far, the Lou Kramer/Jonas Clement case was having an upside.

I got on the blower early. The RTA employee who risked her job for me, and no doubt quite a few others, gave me the details on the BMW. It was owned by Top Fleet Ltd and leased to the Oceania Securities Corporation.

'Car pool,' I said. 'Dead end individual-wise.'

'I'll walk the extra mile for the extra smile.'

We were both on pay phones, and if anyone out there or in there was picking us up then democracy as we know it is dead.

'Walk.'

'Registered driver is Barclay Greaves, 34 Ralston Place, Manly. Usual. Over and out.'

She likes to think of herself as some sort of undercover agent in the service of God knows what. Why not? We all have to get our kicks.

I'd never heard of the company, nor of Greaves, but it was at least interesting that he was apparently in the big money game and lived in the same neck of the woods as Clement.

Rudi Szabo's boxing operation is a complex affair. He trains and manages fighters and promotes fights. You might think this would also promote conflicts of interest and you'd be right in spades. But conflicts of interest are an integral part of the boxing game. Way back in the bare knuckle days, the connections of fighters took side bets on their opponents and boxers themselves did the same. In the modern era, managers have sacrificed one fighter in order to promote another as a regular manoeuvre. Whatever tricks and trade-offs remained in the much-reduced boxing scene in Australia, Rudi was a master of. And worse—throw in loan sharking and receiving. He employed people like the Maori ex-footballer Steve Kooti, whose name had come up as a counsellor at the Liston community protection centre, to collect debts and punish competitors. Luckily, Szabo owed me a favour because I'd happened to save one of his genuinely good fighters from getting into a cut-glass brawl in a Rockdale pub.

I drove to Rudi's establishment in Marrickville—a failed supermarket he'd converted to a gym and offices. It was close to the municipal swimming pool, so Rudi had the use of an extra training facility for free. Rudi had no listed numbers and didn't give the unlisted ones out—you wanted him, you went to see him. I parked and went through the automatic door to the reception area, which just managed to present a businesslike front with a guy behind a desk and a few meaningless framed certificates on the walls. I gave the guy my card and said I wanted to see Rudi.

'What's your business?'

'Rudi knows me, and my business. Tell him I'm collecting on the favour I did him.'

He went away, came back quickly, and took me down a short passage to an office that was within earshot and smell of the gym. The unmistakable sound of a heavy bag being hit and the equally recognisable tang of sweat and liniment were in the air like smoke and the click of balls in a pool room.

Rudi met me at what would've been the door to his office if it'd had a door. It didn't.

'Good to see youse, Hardy. Come on in.'

Rudi is a first generation Australian about whom nothing verbal of the previous generations of foreigners lingers. He looks like a Serb or a Croatian or whatever his antecedents were, with the thickset physique, aggressive moustache and balding bullet head, but he speaks broad Australian.

I shook his meaty hand and took a seat while he put his big bum on his desk, closer to me and higher than he would have been on a chair behind it. I guessed that this was one of his managerial negotiating positions.

'You done me a good turn with Ricky that night. I said it, an' I meant it. So what d'you want? Tickets? No problem.'

'Information. You remember Steve Kooti, used to work for you in an . . . executive capacity?'

The hooded Balkan eyes suddenly brightened as if the brain behind them had just processed a lot of information and gone on the alert.

'Stevie? Yeah, sure. What?'

'Tell me about him.'

'Why?'

'Look, Rudi, I'm not interested in past history. I don't care what he used to do for you when he was one of your frighteners. I want to know what changed him and what you make of him now.'

That relaxed him. He got off the desk and moved around to his chair. He didn't move in the loose way ex-athletes do, he moved stiffly, like a man used to carrying heavy things. Rudi had started out as a builder's labourer.

'Silly cunt got religion. He ran into some religious freaks and they grabbed him. Dunno how. I've always been a Catholic. Doesn't get in the way of nothin' if you don't let it. But this mob Stevie took up with—can't do this, can't do that. Can't take a piss without thanking God for giving you a prick. Tried preaching that crap to me and I told him where he could put it. In the old days an insult like that and he'd have left me under this desk. And I mean *under*! But now it's, "Bless you, brother". Bullshit.'

'He's tied in with some people out Campbelltown way. A community protection outfit. Know anything about them?'

'Coconuts?'

'Islanders, yeah.'

'I've heard of them. There's a few around. I'm told they've got things going.'

'Like?'

He shrugged his beefy shoulders. 'Insurance scams, immigration scams. Shit, I dunno.'

'Doesn't sit too well with praising the Lord.'

'That's fair dinkum for some, just a bloody front for others—the smart ones.'

'What category would Kooti be in?'

'Dunno. I'm fast losing interest in this, Hardy.'

'Fair enough. One last thing—d'you know how I can get in touch with him?'

He smiled, showing a couple of gold-filled teeth, opened a drawer in the desk and rummaged in it. 'Gave me his mobile number in case I wanted to discuss admitting Jesus to my life. Know what I said?'

I shook my head.

'I said, "Sounds like a Mex Bantam. Has he got a left hook?" I thought that was funny. What d'you reckon?'

'Pretty funny.'

He pushed a drink coaster across the desk. 'Here you go. I don't need it. We was havin' a drink—I was, he wasn't.'

I took the coaster, pocketed it and stood. 'Thanks.'

'We square now, Hardy?'

'Sure. Will I say hello from you when I talk to Steve?'

'Okay. Maybe he could put in a good word for me with God.'

'Do you believe in God?'

'Sometimes—when one of my boys gets up off the floor and kayos the other guy.'

'You're all heart, Rudi.'

He waved his arms, embracing the room, the smells, everything. 'Look, I own this place. Got a block of units in Earlwood, a nice home in Strathfield with the missus and the kids, holiday place in Thirroul. Of course I believe in God.'

'How're you going to vote?'

'How do you reckon?'

12

I drove to the office and did a web search on Oceania Securities. It had a website that told me about as little as it could. Investments . . . consultancy . . . portfolio management—that kind of thing. The office was in St Leonards. There were no details given about Barclay Greaves and a web check on him turned up nothing. The *Sydney Morning Herald* database did better. A couple of stories on Greaves came up. He'd been a consultant in a big company merger that had threatened to go bottom up and he was credited with righting it. He was described as forty-six, married with two children, a former tax office heavyweight turned merchant banker turned big-time fixit guy. The article implied that his consultancy fee took a decent bite from both of the merging companies. Good one.

The other piece dealt with his involvement in a New Zealand land deal thrown into doubt by a couple of the parties suddenly coming under fire for tax transgressions. Oceania Securities had arranged amnesties and compromises and the deal had gone through satisfactorily. This item revealed that Greaves was a lawyer with degrees from the universities of Melbourne and Chicago. It was unclear whether he was a New Zealander or an Australian. He described himself as an Australasian to the reporter who'd managed the briefest of interviews,

That was something to chew on. Clearly he had some connection with Clement and not an altogether happy one from his behaviour on party night. Was he backing Lou Kramer's work in some way? He looked like a possible source for the extra money she might need to lure Billie, but what would his motive have been for that? True love? I doubted it.

Given the apparent scale of his operations, I was surprised Greaves hadn't attracted more press attention. But I suppose that just as those who seek it can get it, those who don't want it can avoid it. I had a contact at the *Australian Financial Review,* a former editor in fact, who now had gone back to investigative work as any dinkum journalist would. I rang her and put the question about Greaves.

A true reporter, her first response was, 'Why? Have you got something?'

'Hey, Lily, I'm asking you.'

'Pity. Mystery man, probably an Enzedder but I've never seen his passport. A lot of these types have a few anyway.'

'He's a type, is he?'

'Cliff, I really don't know. There're rumours about him. He's involved in this, he's involved in that, but never anything substantial and he's sort of not interesting enough for anyone to put in the time and effort on him.'

'Is that because he likes it that way?'

'You're learning.'

'What about his politics?'

'No idea. You're intriguing me.'

Lily Truscott is a woman I wouldn't mind intriguing. I'd met her at a fight night in Marrickville. Her brother was on the bill and I was sitting next to her. She was his most enthusiastic supporter, and when I made a few complimentary remarks about his work, she gave me a smile. When he won she jumped up, whooped and gave me a hug.

After that, we had a drink and, as the Stones put it, spent a few nights together. But she was career oriented. So was I, in my way, but there was something there, and I suppose it was in the back of my mind to develop it when I rang her.

'Tell you what, Lil. If anything comes of this I'll let you in on it.'

'Yeah, yeah. But I'll hold you to that and give you this—from what I've heard about Greaves, which is bugger-all, so this is just intuitive stuff, I'd guess that he's a man out to make a big score.'

We left it there. I felt like one of those con men who sell off acres they hold a shaky title to, over and over and over again. But I just might be able to make good on the deal.

The online bank showed that Lou's cheque had bounced and that my account had been debited for the dishonoured fee. I rang and told them to re-present it and that I'd pay the fee to accelerate the clearance again. Hardy the gambler.

That left me with Steve Kooti. A knock came on the door. I opened it and Tommy stood there, uncertain but optimistic.

'Hey, man, you owe me a hundred bucks.'

I had to laugh. 'So I do.' I felt for my wallet but discovered that I didn't have enough cash. 'Have to go to an ATM.'

I pulled the door closed and we started down the stairs. On the way I told him I hadn't meant to run out on him, it was just that I had to follow someone. 'Anyway, I didn't get you in trouble. I didn't go near the house you showed me. How did you find me, by the way?'

'Found one of your cards in the car.'

'So you can go back and get on with your job hunting.'

'Kinda like it down here.'

'Hard without money.'

There was a queue at the ATM and just for something to say I asked him if he knew Steve Kooti.

'I should. He's my uncle.'

I looked at him sharply. 'I thought you were a Koori.'

'Koori one side, Maori the other, with other stuff thrown in. Real mongrel, me.'

I got the cash and gave him the hundred. 'Hang on. I'll buy you a drink.'

He shrugged his acceptance and we went to the pub near the railway station. His was a schooner of New and mine was a middy of light. He took a long drink and sighed. 'That's good. Pity I'm out of smokes.'

I gave him a twenty and he came back with a packet and lighter. 'I'll buy the next round,' he said.

'We'll see. Tell me about Steve. He used to be a heavy, now I'm told he's in the God squad. Does he hang out with Manuma's lot, the protection mob?'

'Shit, no. Used to, but now he's in the other church. Big John's Island Brotherhood, Uncle Steve's in Children of Christ.'

'What's the difference?'

Tommy sucked in smoke and beer. 'Not much as to singing and praying and that, but a lot in other ways.

IB's for coconuts only. Doubt they'd let me in, being part Koori. CC'll take anyone.'

'What else?'

He looked at me shrewdly. 'You're trying to get me in trouble again. Have to pay to do that, man.'

I thought briefly about an idea that had come to me. Tommy had an attitude and some bad habits but he looked strong and he was enterprising. He'd talked about wanting to work. I figured he was worth a chance, especially as he could be useful. 'What if I said I could get you a job here?'

'Doin' what?'

'Gardening, A month's work for sure. Maybe some painting after that.'

'Sounds good. Where?'

'Lilyfield. Friend of mine's bought a rundown house there. Big garden completely overgrown. It needs clearing and straightening up. Then the joint needs painting and repairs. You could doss there while you worked.'

For all his street-wise toughness there was suddenly a bit of vulnerability about him. The thought of having somewhere to live, a real job to do, a place in the scheme of things, seemed to change him from a passenger to something more positive.

'You dinkum?'

'Yes. Course if you fucked up . . .'

His cigarette had burned out and he hadn't lit another. His beer was getting warm. 'I won't. What was it you wanted to know?'

'Let's get this fixed up first.'

Mike D'Angelo, who operates a bottle shop in King Street, is a friend. He'd bought the Lilyfield tumbledown and intended to live there, but with three shops to care for he hadn't the time to clear the block—round about a third of an acre. He'd asked me if I knew a reliable handyman. I bought Tommy a new pair of jeans and a clean T-shirt and he tidied himself up in the little bathroom in my building. I took him to meet Mike and they got along well. Mike handed Tommy the keys to an old ute he had parked behind his shop.

'You'll have to dump lots of loads. Keys to the house and a couple of sheds are on the ring.'

'Right,' Tommy said.

Mike handed over forty dollars. 'Two fifty a week. This comes out of it. You'll need boots and gloves. There's some tools in the ute. Power's on and the phone's connected, I think.'

'Right . . . thanks.'

'I'll show him the place,' I said.

'Watch out for snakes.'

'My totem, man.'

Mike laughed. 'Bullshit.'

'Right,' Tommy said.

We bought work boots and gloves in a disposal store and I drove to the Lilyfield place with Tommy following in the ute. It was a corner block near a park and every weed and noxious growth in the area, native and introduced, had invaded and taken hold. The land was choked with lantana and bougainvillea and wisteria and others I couldn't identify. Tommy took a look and sucked in a breath.

'Whew, big job.'

'You up to it?'

'You bet.'

'He's paying you two fifty a week and free rent. You're looking at a couple of grand easy.'

'I'm grateful, man. Best thing that's happened to me in a long time.'

'Good. Mike runs a pretty big operation—he's got a couple of shops and he's got interests in other businesses. Play your cards right and you could have a career with him.'

Tommy nodded.

'Let's have our talk and I'll leave you to it.'

Tommy Larrigo told me, in his own words, that there was ongoing tension between the Island Brotherhood and the Children of Christ and those attached to both organisations. Now that he was out of the area, he felt free to say that the Brotherhood, while providing some community services, also had a dark side—assisting the Department of Housing and real estate agents in evictions and taking bribes to stave off evictions. As Rudi Szabo had said, there was an insurance scam industry in Liston and adjoining suburbs and it had to be controlled by someone. He'd assumed Steve Kooti was somehow connected with it, but Tommy assured me that the criminal element in the island community was a worry to his uncle, who'd had more than one confrontation over it with John Manuma and others.

I helped Tommy unload the tools from the ute and unlocked the house and the sheds where there were more tools, rusty and cobwebbed but useable. His enthusiasm mounted with each discovery. The power was on in the house but the phone wasn't connected. I gave him my mobile and asked him to call his uncle and arrange a meeting between him and me.

Tommy laid it on thick—how I'd got him this great job

with prospects and what a good guy I was and how he wouldn't be hanging around Liston with his arse out of his pants anymore.

After a few exchanges, some of them in Maori, Tommy shut off the phone and handed it back. 'Says he'll meet you at the Campbelltown TAFE—Narellan Road. He's doing some sort of course there. Says he'll know you. This arvo, two o'clock.'

'Okay,' I said, 'start slashing.'

As I'd told Sharon Marchant, in this game you never know where you're going to be or for how long. I went home, collected the .38 and packed a few clothes and bits and pieces. I tanked up and was on the road south-west again with plenty of time to meet Kooti, racking up the kilometres and petrol receipts against an as yet still unpaid retainer. I'd heard of Kooti over the years from various people but as far as I knew I'd never met him. Still, if he said he'd know me I guessed he would. My plan was simple—to see if I could persuade him to help me detach Billie Marchant from the Island Brotherhood. If I had to put up with some Bible-bashing to achieve that, I would.

Kooti wasn't hard to spot. At about 200 centimetres and a hundred plus kilos, he stood out like a bishop on a beach. He wore a polo shirt with the arm bands stretched to breaking point by his biceps, and baggy shorts that showed the kind of legs that had made him virtually impossible to knock down on a football field. Massive head, a metre of shoulder breadth. I parked and approached him, noting the backpack and book in his hand.

'Mr Hardy,' he said. 'Good to meet you.'

My hand got briefly swallowed up by his. 'Mr Kooti, thanks for agreeing to see me.'

'Good reasons. C'mon over here and sit down. There's a scrap of shade.'

We walked across to where a straggly tree threw some shade over a park bench. He stuffed the book into his backpack; I caught the word 'faith' in the title.

'Tommy said you'd know me, and you did. Can't see how.'

'Ah, doubting Thomas. I'm grateful for what you're doing for him. He's not a bad kid, but wasting his life like so many of them. Maybe you've helped him onto a new path. Yes, I know you. I was there in the Rockdale Arms when you hauled Ricky Clitheroe out of harm's way. I asked who you were later.'

I shrugged. 'He was a lightweight, junior welter at most. All the rest were heavies.'

'I was one of them.' He extended his arms and I could see pale scars crossing the dark skin of his forearms. 'One of the brawlers. I got badly cut up.'

'When you were working for Rudi Szabo?'

'Yes.' He looked at the cheap watch on his wrist just below the scars. 'I've got a class soon. What do you want from me? You know that I'm a servant of the Lord now. I don't do violence.'

I outlined my problem to him, stressing that Billie Marchant needed proper medical care, but not concealing the fact that I had a particular agenda quite apart from her welfare. There was no point in dissembling. Steve Kooti was an impressive piece of work—calm, intelligent, confident. He had the kind of composed inner strength I'd seen in some soldiers, some boxers, some cops and an occasional criminal. You can't bullshit them.

He heard me out. 'John Manuma is a . . . let us say, conflicted man. There is much good about him. He's a genuine Christian, I believe, but his power and influence can send him in wrong directions at times.'

'Do you have any influence with him?'

'No, not of the kind you require. Are you sure this woman is not receiving proper care? The power of prayer and faith are enormous.'

'Her sister says not. She also fears for the boy, her nephew, falling under the influence of this Yoli.'

'Yolande Potare. Yes, he's a different thing altogether. A criminal. I might be able to help you. Have to think about it, and take counsel with others. Where will you be this evening?'

'Wherever you want me to be.'

He looked at me and a smile played across his broad, dark face. 'I don't see you booking into the YMCA. Find a motel in Campbelltown and ring me on the mobile around six o'clock. I have to go.' He slung his backpack, smoothly uncoiled his huge body and moved away. Then he turned back. 'How's Rudi?'

'As ever.'

He nodded. 'Not the worst villain around.'

'What're you studying?' I asked.

'What do you think?'

'Religion?'

He smiled. 'Stereotypical thinking. I'm disappointed in you. Computing, Mr Hardy. Computing.'

People can change, you see it all the time. Religion is one of the great life-changing forces, I have to admit, and not always for the better—think of George Bush. Being given responsibility and some support can work, too, as in Tommy's case. If that held.

The wide open sky I'd noticed in Picton was here as well, wider even, and I felt an impulse to walk under it. The sun went behind a cloud as I wandered over to a basketball court where a pick-up game was in progress. Black and white kids, male and female on both teams. Encouraging. I never cared much for basketball because the professionals score too readily, just as in soccer they don't score enough. But at this level it was more entertaining with a lot of misses and fumbles and no hopped-up coach shouting from the sidelines. A player jumped, threw and missed and the ball came towards me at speed. I caught it and tossed it back.

A kid shouted, 'Wanna play, mister?'

I grinned and shook my head, but the invitation did me a power of good.

13

I checked in to the Three Ways Motor Inn in Campbelltown, phoned Kooti and left the message. That gave me time on my hands. I phoned Sharon Marchant's mobile and she came through as clearly as though she was next door.

'Hey,' she said, 'this is a good connection. Where are you?'

I told her and added that I might have made some progress at getting her sister away from Yoli and Co.

'That's great. Look, I'm with Sarah for a while but I'll be dropping her back home before heading out to Picton. Why don't we get together and you can tell me all about it.'

She agreed to come by the motel in a couple of hours. I inspected the mini-bar. There were three double serves of gin and plenty of tonic water. I went for a walk, located a fruit shop and bought a lemon. A gin and tonic without lemon is like a martini without an olive. I had a swim in the motel pool and was freshly shaved, showered and shampooed when Sharon turned up.

She dropped into a chair and breathed an exhausted sigh. 'Keeping up with the young is the pits. That kid's been running me ragged.'

She was wearing the clothes Lou Kramer had left her and, not flattering to start with, they were wrinkled and shapeless. Her face was aglow with parental happiness but just below that surface she was deeply tired. I put my thoughts of a close encounter aside and made her a drink.

'Thanks. Just one. Two'd put me on my ear and I've got to drive home. Got that class tomorrow. What's been going on, Cliff?'

In fact, I didn't really have much to tell her but I made the most of it, saying that I had an ally among the Liston Islanders and expected to make progress.

'If we get her out I hope you'll be standing by to talk to her.'

She sipped her drink. 'I'd need some assurances about that woman you're dealing with first. Some firm arrangements, unnegotiable, if you know what I mean.'

I said I did. We talked a bit more and she took off to Picton after saying she'd mail the clothes back to me. I knocked off one of the little gins. Thought about ringing Lou Kramer, decided against. I was thinking about dinner when Steve Kooti showed up. He refused alcohol, naturally, so we went to sit by the pool in the evening air, me with a beer and him with a can of coke, as a full yellow moon rose.

'I talked to my sister. She's a nurse in the area health service. It seems she's had a report about a seriously ill woman at that address.'

'That right?'

'Yes. And she's going to pay the place a visit tomorrow. She'll have a couple of paramedics with her who just happen to be members of our congregation.'

'Big blokes?'

'Very big. Understand, if she finds the woman in good health and getting reasonable treatment there's nothing she can do. But if it's not like that she'll have her removed to Western District hospital.'

'Fair enough. What about Yoli?'

'Yoli's going to be busy.'

'I see. This sister, would she be Tommy Larrigo's mother by any chance?'

'No. She's his aunt. I've got a few sisters. Tommy's mother died young, kidney cancer. His father comes and goes. Mary and the others tried to steer him right—I was off being a tough guy as you know—but he was a wild kid.'

'Is there anything I can do?'

'Yes, Mr Hardy. You can stay well clear of everything until you hear from me, one way or the other.'

I agreed to that. We sat in companionable silence for a while as the mozzies buzzed around us and the traffic noise died down. I asked him if he missed it all.

'What?'

'The football. The booze. The fun.'

He laughed. 'Yes, I do. Of course I do. I spent my early years in that atmosphere and loved it. Then I saw the light. I miss it, sure, but I'd never go back to it. Still . . .'

'Still?'

'Maybe you're giving me a little taste of it again. Goodnight, Mr Hardy.'

'Cliff. Goodnight.'

The lights came on around the pool and one situated down below the surface. The water took on an intense blue as midges danced in the light. Then a couple of young guests came into the pool area and jumped in with shouts and splashes and broke my mood. Just as well; it was veering towards self-pity. I gathered up the empty cans and went back to my room. Gaps in the car park showed that only about half of the rooms were occupied. Slow night in Campbelltown under a full moon. Maybe Fisher's ghost would be out.

Experience had taught me how to kill a dead night away from home. A long walk to raise the appetite, a meal with a book, and back to a combination of print and television. 'Media Watch' named and nailed the usual suspects. I read a few chapters of Craig Macgregor's book on Mark Latham and topped it off with a few entries from *1000 Great Lives*, a paperback I'd picked up cheap. The title was misleading; Darwin, one of my heroes, was certainly worth his spot and likewise Muhammed Ali. Hard to see Hitler's life as great, and some were downright miserable—Elvis, for example.

I've never been keen on doing as I was told. Nine o'clock the next morning found me in Liston, parked well away from the house where Billie was staying but with a good view of it through my binoculars. After a few minutes a big Islander dressed in a dark suit left the house, got in one of several cars parked nearby and drove away. Ten minutes later an ambulance pulled up and a white-clad nurse and two paramedics went inside the house. A few more minutes went by and one of the paramedics came out to the ambulance and collected a stretcher.

Looks promising, I thought.

My mobile rang. 'I'm in a phone box. 'Just wanted you to know I was on the job,' Tommy Larrigo said. 'Making progress, man.'

'That's good to know. I'll come by when I get a chance.'

'Finding some strange things here. Old statues of men and women doin' it.'

'Close your eyes,' I said.

I rang off as the paramedics carried the stretcher out with a small blanket-wrapped figure on it. The nurse emerged a little later, scribbling on something attached to a clipboard. She got into the ambulance and it drove away. A smooth operation, but slightly worrying because it meant that Billie Marchant was genuinely unwell. I rang Lou Kramer, got her voicemail, and left the briefest of messages to say where I was staying and what I was doing. Then I rang Sharon Marchant.

'What?' she snapped.

I told her Billie was on her way to the hospital.

'Shit, I've got a class in ten minutes.'

'Ring the hospital. Tell them you'll be there as soon as you can. Someone from the family should be there.'

'I'll get Sarah to go. She's never met her but she's her niece, after all. I'll get there later this morning. Where will you be?'

'I'll be there.'

She laughed. 'I'll tell her to look out for you. Sarah'll be glad to meet you. She's sure we're on together.'

'They think of nothing else.'

The ambulance didn't use its siren on the way to the hospital, a sign that Billie wasn't at death's door. It took a while for me to find a parking place and then to locate the admissions desk. I enquired about Ms Billie Marchant and was told she'd been admitted by Sister Mary Latekefu of the District Health Service. She was receiving treatment for malnutrition, dehydration and pneumonia and couldn't receive visitors until a doctor said so.

I moved away from the desk and a young woman who'd been standing nearby approached me. She was medium tall, slim, brown haired, olive skinned—Sharon without the dye job, a few shades darker and twenty years younger.

'Mr Hardy?'

'You'd be Sarah . . . Marchant?'

'Sarah Marchant-Wallambi. Didn't Mum tell you? My dad's a Koori.'

'Glad to meet you, Sarah. Did you hear all that about your Aunt Billie?'

She smiled as we moved away towards a set of plastic chairs. 'Yeah, except that she's Aunty Wilhelmina. That's her real name. I was just going to ask about her when you stepped in.'

'I'm finding out more about your family all the time,' I said. 'How much d'you know about what's going on?'

'Not much. I know she's a wild one and into drugs and all that. I met her once when I was a kid. That's when she told me her name. I thought she was great, but Mum didn't like to talk about her much.'

I bought us two coffees from the machine and we sat on the hard chairs they provide with arm rests so you can't stretch out on a few of them for a nap. She dropped her backpack to the floor and drank some coffee. She was wearing jeans and a T-shirt, sandals. She had a couple of rings in her ears but none in her face. 'Can you tell me what this's all about? I mean, suddenly Mum's in Sydney with a strange man and her car needs picking up and her sister's off to hoppy and you're here . . . like, this is so un-my mum.'

'It's a long story. Billie . . . Wilhelmina . . . she's a sort of witness in something pretty big to do with money and other stuff. I'm working for someone who needs to talk to her and can help her to pull out of this bad patch she's in. Your mother's on side more or less, if we can work out the details.'

'Wow. Is she in danger . . . Billie?'

'Not while she's here. Look, what you should do is tell them you're her niece and that her sister's on the way. Tell Sharon I'm going off to organise my client to see Billie when she's well enough. Okay?'

She nodded. I patted her shoulder. She gave me a look I'd seen before on the faces of wise children of women I'd got involved with. Is this guy a candidate? With the scars, the broken nose, the manners for the moment and the secrets? Probably not.

I gave Sarah the motel number and headed back there expecting a visit or at least a call from Steve Kooti to put me in the picture. I also wanted to think about how to play things with Lou Kramer. Her bull-at-a-gate style wasn't right for things as they stood, and I worried that negotiations between her and Sharon could easily break down. Still, I considered I wasn't doing too badly so far, with Billie found and secured and an ally or two on the side. I stopped for petrol and, as I hadn't eaten anything yet and felt I owed myself an indulgence, I had a cup of coffee and a sandwich at the servo.

I pulled in to the motel car park and hoped they weren't doing my room. Nothing more boring than kicking your heels while they cart out the empties. But the door was closed and there was no sign of the trolley. I went in and something about the weight of a Mack truck hit me on the back. My knees crumpled; a skyhook picked me up and dumped me on the bed. I fought for breath, waiting for the next assault, but nothing happened. With almost everything hurting, I wrenched myself around to see a man standing beside the bed. He was so big he blocked out most of the light from the window. He wore the kind of high buttoning single-breasted suit that footballers wear to the tribunal and their court hearings. I recognised him as the man I'd seen leaving the Liston house that morning. Had to be Yolande Potare.

He cracked his knuckles with a noise like the rattle of small arms fire. 'You're a nuisance,' he said, 'and I don't like you.'

'Doing my job.'

'Interfering with the Lord's work.'

'You reckon the Lord likes to see sick women wasting away to death, do you? She's where she belongs, Mr Potare. Let it be.'

'I will. But first I'm going to make you sorry you ever got born. Stand up.'

The bedside lamp was anchored, and the clock radio; the only weapon to hand was a pillow. I slung it at him as I stood, hoping to distract him long enough to pick up something solid or, better still, get through the door. He swatted it away, grabbed me by the shoulder and drew back his other arm to totally rearrange my face.

The door burst open and two men came in. They weren't as big as Yoli but one was big enough. He grabbed Yoli's arm and swung him off balance while the other guy kneed him in the crotch. Yoli released me, bellowed with pain and rage and bent double. The smaller man flashed something in a leather folder under Yoli's eyes.

'If you want to be up on assault charges, you can be,' he said.

His mate took a handful of Yoli's suit collar and pulled him towards the open door as Yoli was still fighting for breath. 'Or you can just piss off.'

Yoli staggered through as he was released and the door was kicked shut behind him. I sat down on the bed and massaged my shoulder.

'Police?'

The big man dusted his hands off, looking pleased with himself. 'No. My name's McGuinness and this is . . . well, never mind. We work for someone who's anxious to meet you.'

'Look, I'm glad you happened along. Don't quite see how but—'

'That can be explained. Just stay put.'

I took a closer look at him. McGuinness was big, fair, freckled and running to fat. His exertions had left him short of breath. His mate was more compact, possibly smarter, but not in charge. Both had something like an ex-army or ex-cop poise I didn't like the look of, but there was no point in arguing.

McGuinness opened the door and gestured invitingly. I heard a car door slam and footsteps approaching on the concrete path. Leather soles, confident tread. McGuinness held the door wide open and Barclay Greaves walked in.

14

Greaves, looking like John Cleese with a gut, sat in the room's only comfortable chair. He would. McGuinness's mate opened the fridge, poured a glass of water and handed it to me.

'How're you feeling, Mr Hardy?' Greaves said.

I drank some water. 'I'm okay, Mr Greaves.'

He glanced at McGuinness. 'Did you mention my name?'

McGuinness shook his head.

'No mystery,' I said. 'I saw you in the company of Louise Kramer the other night. Checked your car registration and Bob's your uncle. We sort of met at Jonas Clement's party, if you remember.'

'Yes, indeed. Well, I'm impressed. Wasn't that a bit above and beyond the call of duty? Keeping tabs on your own client?'

'Can't be too careful. I knew she wasn't giving me the full picture.'

'I'm not sure anyone knows what precisely that is. Louise is devious. That's all right, so am I, and you seem to have acquired some formidable enemies. I'm told Rhys

Thomas gave you a hard time, and that big chap certainly wasn't friendly.'

'True. Well, your blokes helped me out there. I suppose I should be grateful.'

He nodded. He was immaculate in his suit, muted striped shirt and silk tie. His colour was a few shades too high and he was carrying those extra kilos. One-on-one I didn't think he'd give me much trouble, but the presence of the other two tipped the balance.

'Yes,' Greaves said. 'That should put us on a good footing, wouldn't you say?'

'All depends on what you want.'

He looked uncomfortable in the surroundings. Cheap motel rooms weren't his milieu and I felt encouraged because they were mine. McGuinness and his mate were standing around awkwardly. I got off the bed, picked up the pillow I'd thrown at Yoli and pulled out the plastic chair from the tiny desk. I reversed it, sat with my elbows on the back rest and faced Greaves. A quick nod was all he needed to dismiss his minions. They left the room without looking at me.

'Good at what they do,' Greaves said.

'Yeah. Be interesting if that big bastard's out there waiting for them.'

'I imagine they'll cope. What d'you know about me?'

'I'm expecting a phone call on my mobile,' I said. 'It's in the car. How about one of your blokes fetches it for me? It's in my jacket on the back seat. The back passenger side door doesn't lock properly. He can jiggle it open.'

He studied me for some seconds, shrugged, took a mobile not much bigger than a fountain pen from his jacket pocket and made a call. A few minutes later the door opened and a hand tossed the mobile at me. I caught it and the door closed.

'Not real polite,' I said.

'Let's stop pissing around. As you'll have gathered I'm . . . backing Louise's book.'

'Nice way of putting it.'

'Don't be a smartarse, Hardy. I can make life very difficult for you if I wish.'

I went to the fridge, took out a can of beer and cracked it. 'I'm sure you can,' I said. 'People with lots of money will try to do that. Trouble is, what they do sometimes comes back to bite them. Why don't you just tell me what your interest in this thing is and I'll decide whether to accommodate you, which at the moment looks unlikely, or to give the whole case the flick or maybe . . . even . . . play it some other way.'

'You're a nuisance. I advised Louise against hiring you.'

I shrugged and swigged some beer. 'You win some, you lose some. I found Billie. Cut her loose.'

'You did. I daresay I would have managed it in time, but I'll give you the credit. Now, I'll lay my cards on the table. I detest Jonas Clement and I'm willing to move heaven and earth to bring him down.'

'I got the feeling you weren't pals the other night. What did he do to you?'

'Never mind. I want to know what this woman knows about the killing of Eddie Flannery and everything else.'

I shrugged. 'We're a fair way off from that still. First, Billie has to be well enough and in her right mind enough to be talked to. Then her sister has to be convinced it's in her best interest to talk. For all I know, Billie might want to go back to singing hymns with the Islanders in Liston.'

Greaves looked annoyed. 'I understood it was mainly a matter of money—getting the right treatment for the woman.'

'Maybe, maybe not.'

'Why do I get the feeling you're being deliberately obstructive?'

I lowered the level in the can. I was almost enjoying myself. 'Why do I have the suspicion you might be planning to blackmail Clement? I don't give a rat's arse about him, but I've dealt with enough people of your stamp to know that they play a rough game by no known rules when it comes to business.'

'You're right there. But criminal charges against Clement'll serve my purpose well enough. All I ask is that I be present when this woman talks . . . Billie.'

'Wilhelmina.'

'What?'

'That's her name, Wilhelmina.'

'You're an annoying man, Hardy.'

'Well, I'm annoyed myself. I told Lou to keep everything under her hat and she's been filling you in.'

'As I said, I'm subsidising her work.'

'I hope you've subsidised enough to cover my retainer cheque. It bounced.'

He shook his head. 'Silly girl.'

'I wouldn't say that. Are you sure she's playing your game or one of her own?'

'Good point. We'll have to see, won't we? You're in my debt. That Polynesian would have hurt you badly. Someone still might.'

'A threat?'

'A warning. I'll be in touch through Louise.'

He'd adjusted the creases in his trousers when he'd sat down. He readjusted them now as he stood and moved to the door. I rubbed my bruised shoulder and drained the can as he left. He was right about this case making me more enemies than I needed—Manuma, Potare, Clement and his son, and Rhys Thomas, Greaves and his helpers and, for all I knew, Lou Kramer herself. My allies so far were Sharon Marchant, Tommy Larrigo and Steve Kooti. No contest. At least the only gun around was mine.

I went out to the car to check that the gun was as safe as it could be given the dodgy door. The Falcon slumped like a drunk; all four tyres had been slashed and the car was settled on the hubs.

'Yoli,' I said.

A car pulled into the area and, just as I spoke, Steve Kooti got out accompanied by a woman in nurses' uniform. They joined me by the stricken car.

'Did I hear you say Yoli?' Kooti said.

'That's right. He was here.'

Kooti examined me closely. 'That eye wasn't thumped today. Yoli doesn't seem to have done you any damage. I'm surprised.'

'He was prevented. I expect this is Nurse Latekefu.' I held out my hand.

'Sister Latekefu,' Kooti said.

She shook my hand vigorously. She was a big, solidly built woman with a firm grip. 'Tch, Stephen, it doesn't matter. I'm glad to meet you, Mr Hardy.'

'Thanks for what you've done, Sister. How is she?'

'Not well. She was in a coma or very close to it. That

house was in a dreadful state, I'm ashamed to say. It's not like our people to live that way.'

'They're not our people,' Kooti said.

'You know they are, Stephen. They're just on a wrong path.'

I pointed to my room. 'Would you like to come in? I could make some coffee or something.'

'Thank you, no,' Mary Latekefu said. 'We just wanted to make sure you were all right. John Manuma said that Yoli Potare was very angry and he's a violent man. Somebody told him they'd seen your car in Liston and following us to the hospital.'

'I'd back Steve here against him.'

'I'm non-violent these days, Mr Hardy,' Kooti said.

I looked at my car and non-violence wasn't the note I wanted to strike. I unlocked the car and took the .38 from the glove box, holding it low and out of sight of passers-by but not of them. They looked dismayed.

'I won't kid you,' I said, 'this matter involves some ruthless people. I think it'd be best if you kept your distance from this point on. I think the woman you took to hospital will be okay. I think she can be helped and protected and I'll be trying to do that, but there are complications.'

Mary Latekefu nodded. 'I met her niece. Seemed like a capable young woman.'

'Her mother, the sister, is the same.'

'We've got enough problems in Liston to be going on with,' Kooti said. 'I'm happy to leave this to you but there's one thing I want to say.'

'I can guess,' I said. 'Tommy has to be kept clear of it all.'

'Right.'

'I'll give you the address where he's living and working. I spoke to him this morning and he was hard at it. I'll try to get the phone on there and I'll get the number to you. I can't see how any of this can touch him.'

His nod said, *you'd better be right.* I got my notebook and scribbled down the Lilyfield address. They drove off and I rang the NRMA. After an hour or more, a tow truck arrived and I travelled for free to the nearest garage, but four new tyres were going to cost Lou Kramer and Barclay Greaves a bundle.

I hung about annoying the mechanic by my presence while the tyres were fitted and then drove back to check out of the motel. Some of the comings and goings had been observed and I got the impression they were glad to be rid of me. They didn't even try to charge for a late check-out.

I drove to the hospital and parked even further away than I had the time before and had to contend for the spot with a Volvo. By now it was early afternoon; the day had heated up and dried out and tempers were getting frayed. I made my way to the waiting room for the floor Billie was on and was greeted by several hostile faces—Sarah Marchant-Wallambi, Sharon, who'd re-dyed her hair to a dark brown and looked the more formidable for it, Lou Kramer, in professional suit and heels, and whatever-his-first-name-was McGuinness. Sharon got to her feet and advanced towards me like a one-person SWAT team.

'There you are finally,' she said. 'What the fuck is going on here?'

'Mum!' Sarah said.

'Don't Mum me.' She pointed to Lou and McGuinness. 'What're these two doing here? My sister's in a coma and—'

I wasn't in the mood for this. 'I'll tell you who *should* be here, and that's Mary Latekefu, the nurse who fronted those people who were holding Billie and got her out of there.'

'Well, where is she then?'

'Calm down, Sharon. You'll meet her and you should thank her. She's got other things to do.'

'And you should thank Mr Hardy, Mum. He helped to get Aunt Billie here.'

'Mr Hardy's being paid,' Sharon snapped. 'And what this bloke has to do with things I don't like to think.'

McGuinness straightened his jacket and tie and moved into a comradely stance with Lou Kramer, who was yet to even give me a glance. 'It's safe to say that all of us here are working in Ms Marchant's interest. Albeit perhaps from different angles. I'm in a position to say that when she recovers from her present condition, and I've had an assurance from the medical staff that she will recover, with the permission of her nearest of kin, Ms Marchant, she can be transferred to a private hospital where her every medical and psychological need will be met and paid for.'

Lou nodded but Sharon looked ready to claw her eyes out after disembowelling McGuinness. 'The medicos have told us bugger-all and you say they've talked to you. How come?'

McGuinness shrugged. 'Influence, Ms Marchant. Influence. When it works for you, don't knock it.'

'The question is, who're *you* working for?'

I left them to it and drew Lou Kramer aside. She came, reluctantly. 'You certainly played your cards close to your chest, Lou,' I said.

She shrugged. 'I had to. Barclay didn't want anyone knowing of our association.'

'I knew about it almost from day one. Did you enjoy your dinner at the Malaya the other night?'

Another shrug. 'So you're a detective. So what? I'll admit you did a great job getting hold of Billie. I'd say our business is concluded. Thank you. If you'll submit your account with your expenses . . .'

'That's if your retainer cheque clears.'

'It will.'

'Yeah, with Greaves backing you I suppose so. You don't really think he just wants you to nail Clement in a book, do you?'

'If you knew what Clement had done to him you'd understand.'

'And what would that be?'

'I can't tell you. Thanks for all you did. If I ever need a private detective again—'

'Go elsewhere,' I said and turned away. I'd had enough of her and McGuinness and Greaves, and Sharon Marchant seemed to have had enough of me. She was still locked in dispute with McGuinness, her daughter looking agitated on the sidelines. I would've been glad to see Steve Kooti or Mary Latekefu, who'd been straightforward and effective, but there was no sign of them. I decided to walk away from it all, although I was sure there were loose ends everywhere. But I wouldn't get paid for tying them up even if I could.

The loose ends niggled at me on the drive back to Sydney, but as the kilometres between me and the others increased and I took in the news and some talk programs on the radio, I could feel detachment cutting through. I'd hit my client with the full Monty of an expense account and put the whole thing down to experience.

I took the drive quietly, stopped for a drink and was back in the pollution by late afternoon. There's always a let-down after the end of an assignment and in that mood I need company, not a big empty house creaking around me. I bought a six-pack, drove to Lilyfield and parked outside Mike's dream home to-be. The block had a high privet hedge around three sides, but I could hear signs of activity behind it.

I opened the gate and saw Tommy slashing away at a stand of lantana. He'd already made a good start, clearing some of the weeds and rubbish. He was stripped to the waist and sweat was running down his hard, lean body. He was slamming the machete so hard into the tough stalks that he didn't hear me approach.

'Hey, take it easy. You'll do yourself out of a job.'

He spun around and his grimy, sweat-stained face broke into a wide grin. 'Good to see you, man. What d'you reckon?'

'I reckon you've made a bloody good start and it's time to knock off and have a beer.'

He dug the machete into one of the cut stalks and wiped his face with the back of his hand. 'I'll be in that.'

I tossed him a can and we sat down under a tree on a couple of upturned milk crates.

'Cheers.'

'Geez, that hits the spot.'

We knocked the cans off in rapid time and started on a second, taking it more slowly. He asked me what I'd been doing and I filled him in as much as I felt necessary.

'So you're the one out of a job?' he said.

'Something'll turn up.'

He waved his hand at the yard. 'You could help me here.'

'No thanks, I've done all this sort of yakka I ever want to do.'

'When would that've been, Cliff?'

I thought about it. 'A bit in the army to toughen us up. That was in Queensland. It was about twenty degrees hotter than this. That got the fat off. I've helped a few mates who've bought acreages here and there, over the years.'

'Never fancied it yourself?'

'No fear, I'm a city boy, born and bred and likely to die.'

'Bad vibe to talk about dyin'.' He stood and stretched. 'Reckon I'll put in another hour or so. I tell you what, I'll sleep like a log after this.'

'I'll leave you the tinnies.'

'Just the one,' he said. 'I'm tryin' to cut down on it. Haven't had a smoke today either.'

I laughed. 'Just don't find Jesus.'

'No risk of that.'

'Your Uncle Steve said he might call in here. I think he'd be impressed with what you're doing. Your Aunt Mary as well.'

'She's terrific, isn't she? Tried to keep me at school and that. Too dumb to listen. Bloody hard when all you can see in front of you's the fuckin' work for the dole shit. Hey, that woman in Yoli's house. She goin' to be okay?'

'I guess so.' I detached a can from the plastic and left him one. 'Not my problem anymore. See you, Tommy.'

After a few days, with Lou Kramer's cheque cleared, my account submitted and a few other minor matters taken in hand, I'd convinced myself of what I'd told Tommy. I called in there again and found him still making progress and still enjoying himself. He said his uncle had been by and spoken highly of what he was doing and also of me. Nice to hear.

Lou's second cheque came through in full settlement and this one cleared first off. I was well ahead and, with summer coming on, began to think of taking a holiday. I went to the gym every day, kept away from the fats and felt in pretty good nick. Where to go? I considered the central and north coasts but decided against them. Beaches too crowded; too many yahoos on the roads. I got out a few maps and travel and accommodation guides and worked through them, thinking more about the south coast. The Illawarra was a bit too close, Bermagui a bit too far away. I was thinking about a time I'd spent at Sussex Inlet years ago. Something very attractive about a quiet estuary and a good surf beach in the one location.

The election was looming and, depending on when I got away, I might have to lodge an absentee vote. Or I might just skip the whole thing and take my chances on being fined. With council, state and federal elections coming along regularly and all voting compulsory, it sometimes seemed that democracy was getting out of hand. Maybe five-year terms with no one to sit for more than two terms would be the go. I was sure there were arguments against that, but the thought of time-servers who did nothing but toe the party line and wait to draw their super angered me.

I'd done a year of constitutional law in my aborted law course and enjoyed it more than torts or contracts. I seemed to remember that I'd passed it. It was back when there looked to be possibilities of change in Australia, when change wasn't a dirty word. Now it was all steady as she goes.

I was leafing through the accommodation guide with the Amex card to hand when the phone rang by my elbow. I picked it up, not expecting a prospective client to call at home, but it happens. I was prepared to say I was on holiday.

'Cliff Hardy.'

'Cliff, Cliff, it's Sharon. You have to help me. Billie's disappeared.'

part two

15

Sharon said she wanted to meet in my office and to get everything on a businesslike basis. I said I'd be willing to help without that because I'd never been happy about the way I'd left things.

'No,' she said. 'Those bastards paid twenty thousand dollars into my bank account. They said it was to help Billie get resettled somewhere and then they . . . well, I'll tell you when I see you. But I want to use their fucking money to find her.'

She showed up at the office wearing jeans and a Panthers football shirt, sneakers. Her hair was pulled back in a ponytail and she hadn't bothered with makeup. There were flecks of paint on the jeans and the shirt. She plonked herself down in the client chair.

'I know, I know,' she said. 'I look like shit. Oh, I've got that bitch's clothes in the car.'

'Let's give them to the Smith Family. She's not exactly my favourite person either.'

'I thought you and her might be . . .'

'No. Let's hear it, Sharon. What's happened?'

She told me that Billie had come out of the coma and

that the doctors had pronounced her well enough to be moved to a private hospital for detoxification and treatment for depression. McGuinness had got in touch with Sharon, told her Billie would be moved to the Charlton Private Hospital in Artarmon if she signed a release form he'd fax to her, and that the money would be paid to her directly.

'Dumb little westie me, I didn't question him and I thought, *North Shore, fine.* When I tried to check on the visiting hours I found that there was no record of Billie being admitted. Sarah's upset and I don't like seeing my kid upset.'

'What sort of a place is it?'

'Oh, it's the real McCoy—big, hot and cold running doctors and nurses. I can't see it being involved in anything fishy.'

'You never know.'

I told her about Barclay Greaves being behind Lou Kramer's book and my suspicion that there was more to his interest than just getting the dirt on Jonas Clement. 'He's rich with lots of different interests. Could be he's got a piece of this hospital and could . . . arrange something.'

'Well, that's something for you to look into. It'd be a start at least.'

'What about the police? Abduction's a serious crime.'

She shook her head. 'No way. There're all sorts of warrants out on Billie—for drugs, using and supplying, probably old non-appearance in court things as well. They'd say good riddance.'

'Okay, I'll see what I can find out. But I have to tell you, big money can do all sorts of shitty stuff, cut corners, smooth things out.'

'Yeah, I know. Somehow she got in real deep this time.

I'm facing never seeing her again, I know that. But I feel guilty about what's happened. She was better off with those Polynesians . . .'

'No. She'd have been dead by now.'

'She might be anyway. I feel as if I've been bought off with this money. How the fuck did they know my bank details?'

'As I said, they can do things. But so can I, sometimes.'

She insisted on signing a contract and writing a cheque. I said I'd keep her in the picture if I got anywhere but she shouldn't get her hopes too high.

She left and I reached for the phone. It hadn't seemed diplomatic to mention it to Sharon, but my first port of call was Louise Kramer. I rang the numbers I had for her and got the answer machine at the home number and a not available for the mobile. I found the number for the *Sydney News* in the phone book and rang it.

'News.'

'Louise Kramer, please.'

There was a long pause and then the female voice said, 'Are you trying to be funny?'

'I'm sorry, what . . . ?'

'Haven't you seen today's paper? Louise is dead. She committed suicide the day before yesterday.'

I almost dropped the phone. I don't get the papers delivered because I never know when I'm going to be away or for how long and nothing marks a house out as unoccupied more than a pile of plastic-wrapped papers. I went down to King Street and bought the *Sydney Morning Herald.* The report was on page four. It said that journalist Louise Kramer, thirty-six, had been found dead by the cleaner who arrived on schedule to clean her apartment.

Ms Kramer had been found in bed with a bottle of vodka on the bedside table and an empty vial of sleeping tablets. The police were reported as saying that Ms Kramer had a history of drug abuse and depression, and that the circumstances of her death were not being regarded as suspicious.

Like hell, I thought. I went back to the office and made a succession of phone calls, trading on past favours and associations, until I got on to the detective who'd filed the initial report on Lou's death. His name was Hamilton and he wasn't happy.

'I'm told I should talk to you,' he said. 'Why?'

'Louise Kramer.'

'Suicide, open and shut.'

'Did you know she was working on an exposé of a certain very important person?'

'Hardy, I know blokes like you think you can run rings round blokes like me, but you can stick it up your arse. I talked to the publisher who advanced her twelve grand. She said Kramer was way behind schedule, hadn't met a deadline to turn in a few chapters, and they were just about to write her off. Probably contributed to her depression, which, by the way, I checked with her quack. On and off the pills, self-medicating with booze; classic case. Okay?'

I didn't know him, but I could picture him—cynical, probably misogynistic and homophobic, happy not to have to deal with yet another piece of human misery. Couldn't blame him, they see so much of it. I let him have the last word and hung up. Looking back, I'd seen something of that fragility in Lou, but it hadn't registered strongly. Should have. I'd congratulated myself on finding her association with Barclay Greaves and let it go at that.

I should have probed her professional life more closely.

Check out the client, I'd told the students, but I'd only done half the job. As I sat with the Newtown traffic humming under the window and a hot Sydney day developing, I gave Louise Kramer a respectful nod. She was like a lot of people who get out of their depth in the world where money and power rule—game to the last, but I'd be prepared to bet that the Stoli and those pills had been forced down her unwilling throat.

The two obvious candidates were Clement and Greaves, or rather their muscle men. If what Hamilton had said about Lou's progress with the book was right, she seemed to be less of a threat to Clement than it first appeared. But Clement might not know that. In any case, my brief was to locate Billie and that meant focusing on Greaves. I did a web check on the Charlton Private Hospital but learned nothing useful. As Sharon had said, it looked established and respectable. It'd be difficult to contrive a secret admission and cover-up in such a place. Difficult, but not impossible.

I had Greaves's Manly address, but didn't for a moment imagine he'd have Billie tucked away there. The web told me that Oceania Securities' office was in St Leonards. I drove there, parked, and looked the place over. The company occupied the whole of a narrow, four storey free-standing building in a quiet street a few blocks away from the Royal North Shore Hospital. There were getting to be too many hospitals in the case for my liking. There was a small, three-level car park within a hundred metres of the Oceania building and I saw a number of people come out of the offices, head to the car park and emerge behind the wheel. Client parking. Employee parking, too? It seemed likely.

I fed coins into the parking meter and waited. In my game you have to have the bladder control of the royals and an equal capacity to withstand boredom. Prostate trouble would put you out of business. After a couple of hours my patience was rewarded when McGuinness, wearing a smart tan suit, left the building and walked to the car park. A few minutes later, a silver BMW, the mate to the one I'd seen Greaves driving, rolled out. Had to be him.

I couldn't decide whether McGuinness was ex-army or ex-cop—maybe both; a military policeman? In any case, I knew I'd have to exercise great care in following him. I'd given talks on the subject to the TAFE students, but there aren't really any rules beyond the obvious one of not following too closely as if hooked on to the back bumper. Change lanes if possible, lift and lower the sun visors to effect a minimal change in the look of the car, don't get caught by red lights but don't run them either.

As I drove I reflected that the last tailing job I'd done had been following Sharon to Picton. That was a piece of cake compared to this. McGuinness was a bit of a lead foot, pushing the Beemer up past the speed limit whenever possible, and braking hard when he had to. Wouldn't do the car any good, but then it wasn't his car. We headed west briefly, then north, over the Roseville Bridge and on to Frenchs Forest. I hadn't been up that way for some time and the area had undergone a lot of change with high-price housing estates taking up more space. People have to live somewhere and developers have to make millions.

The traffic thinned and the tailing job got harder and then harder still, threading through the labyrinth of streets. I couldn't afford to stay near enough to keep McGuinness closely in sight all the way and had to rely on catching glimpses as he signalled and turned. Stressful work with the dipping sun reflecting off metal and glass surfaces but I managed it. I just caught the signal as the BMW slid up the driveway to a sprawling two storey house. I stopped within a hundred metres and saw the garage door slide open in response to the remote control. No home should be without one.

There was access to the house through the garage because McGuinness didn't appear again. I sat in the Falcon with its engine ticking as it cooled down and considered my options. There was really only one. I crossed the street, opened the low gate and walked up to the front porch. The house was brick and fairly newly occupied to judge by the state of the garden, struggling to get established in poor soil under the water regulations. The screen door was a semi-security job but not much use since it was unlocked. I swung it open and pressed the buzzer.

Chimes sounded inside and a woman came to the door. She opened it, probably expecting the screen to be between her and anyone calling, but she didn't seem too worried about it.

'Mrs McGuinness?'

'Yes.'

'Is your husband at home? I'd like a word with him.'

She was attractive in a well-worn and slightly brittle way, and, at a guess, ten years younger than McGuinness, who I took to be about forty. She wore beige cargo pants and a black shirt with three strands of gold chain around her neck. My bruises and wounds had pretty much healed up and I was looking respectable enough in drill pants and a blue business shirt. I gave her one of my most reassuring smiles.

'The security door was unlocked,' I said. 'Tch, tch.'

She returned the smile, but only just. 'My fault. Don't tell Clive. He's out by the pool having a drink. Would you like to come through?'

I followed her down the passage, walking on a thick carpet runner over polished boards, past a living room and a couple of bedrooms. We went through the well-appointed kitchen to a door leading to a deck. I could see the evening light glinting on bright blue water. She paused at the door. 'Can I get you a drink?'

'Thank you. I'll have whatever Clive's having.'

There were lights on in the big yard and by the pool. McGuinness was on a chaise beside the pool, talking on his mobile. He was wearing a T-shirt, swimming trunks and was barefooted. The gate was open. I went through without him hearing me, put two hands under the side of the recliner and flipped him into the water. He shouted and came up spluttering, standing in the shallow end. He recognised me and opened his mouth to shout something but I put my finger to my lips and pointed to where his wife was coming from the house. He began feeling in the water for his phone.

'Clive! What on earth are you doing?'

'It's all right, Dottie. I just overbalanced. Dropped my phone.'

'It'll be ruined. Oh, here's your drink, Mr . . . ?'

'Cliff,' I said. 'Thanks. Why don't you get Clive a robe or something, Mrs Mac. I'm afraid we have to talk in private.'

She was suspicious. My manner and tone told her that I wasn't the innocent caller she'd taken me for. She glanced at McGuinness, who nodded, and she went back to the house. McGuinness located the phone, put it on the side of the pool and used the ladder to climb out. Wringing wet, with his hair in his eyes, he'd lost all his poise and smooth competence. He was well built, or had been, but there was a soft look about him—too much sitting down, too many working breakfasts and lunches—and he didn't fancy his chances against me.

Dottie came down the path and tossed a towelling robe to McGuinness, who only just managed to stop it falling into the pool. She turned on her heel and went back to the house. McGuinness took off his T-shirt and pulled on the robe, righted the chaise and sat down. His drink was on the tiles and he picked it up, fighting for composure.

I took a pull on the glass I'd been given. Gin and tonic, a bit weak but very acceptable. 'That's better now, Clive, isn't it?' I said. 'Let's cut to the chase. Where's Billie Marchant?'

'I don't know what you mean.'

'Either you tell me or I toss you in again and hold you under until you do. I might even hold you there a bit too long.'

'You wouldn't.'

I kicked the phone back into the pool. 'I've seen it done by a master. If you judge it right you promote just that little bit of brain damage. Can lead to a stroke later on.'

'Jesus, Hardy.'

'Your choice. That woman was sort of under my protection and I feel bad about her going missing. So do a few other people.'

He finished his drink and maybe thought briefly about throwing the glass at me, but it wasn't really glass, just some kind of heavy plastic, appropriate to poolside drinking.

I sipped my drink, smiled and shook my head. That gesture seemed to take a toll of him and I realised that he was very frightened, more frightened than he should have been by my actions and threats.

'I had nothing to do with it,' he said.

It was almost as if he was taking a polygraph test and confident of giving a right answer, but there was still that fear.

I knew the reason. 'What about Louise Kramer's suicide?'

'Oh, God.'

He ran his hands over his head and the water dripped into his eyes. He scrubbed at them, making himself a picture of misery. This was a man with things on his mind. He lifted his head. 'I saved you from being bashed by that big—'

'That was then, this is now. Since then you've been an accessory to murder and abduction. Things've changed a bit. Of course Greaves could get you a lawyer and he could get you bail and all, but d'you want to take that chance?'

He shook his head.

'Didn't think so. Don't worry, Clive. I'm sure we can do a deal here.'

16

'Does your wife know about the sorts of things you do for Greaves?'

'Leave her out of it.'

'I just want to be sure she doesn't run off and phone up your little mate.'

'She won't.'

'Trouble in Paradise?'

'We're not as close as we were.'

'Too bad. I'm pretty sure I can convince the police Louise Kramer didn't suicide. I can get them to investigate things—phone calls, sightings of cars, purchase of vodka . . .'

He started to speak but I stopped him.

'I don't want to know what you did or didn't do personally. I know you were involved,' I said. 'She lied to me and used me and I don't owe her anything. What I'm interested in is the whereabouts of Billie Marchant.'

'Why?'

'I'm working for her sister now.'

'You're a leech.'

'Poetic. Listen, you'll like this—she's fixing to pay me with the money you gave her to go away.'

'It wasn't like that.'

'She thinks it was and she's not happy about it.'

In the not-so-far distance I heard a car door slam and a metal gate slide open, grinding a little. I looked at McGuinness, who shrugged.

'Dottie's taken herself off somewhere.'

'Like?'

'Don't know, don't care.'

'That's not a good attitude.'

'I knew you were trouble the minute I set eyes on you and I told Barclay so. Get on with it, Hardy. I'm cold and I need another drink.'

'Best to keep you that way. What has Greaves got against Jonas Clement?'

He gave me a shrewd look. 'Don't know everything, do you?'

'I know enough to put you in prison for conspiracy to commit murder and abduction.'

'I could charge you with assault.'

'You fell in, told your wife so.'

He shook his hair and water dripped down into his eyes again. He rubbed them red. 'Shit, this was getting too heavy for me anyway. Will you give me some time to get clear?'

'If I like what you say.'

'I don't suppose you listen to Clement's radio spot?'

'Why would I? Why would anyone?'

'Right, well, about five or six years ago, no, maybe four years, Clement blew the gaff on a deal Barclay was trying to put through. It was a loans thing to some Pacific country, I forget the name. Essentially it was a money laundering operation. Clement had the inside story and exposed it on the air. It didn't make a big splash; his audience wasn't that big then, but it stopped the deal dead. Barclay arranged a quick retreat and cover-up but he lost a lot of money and face.'

'Why'd Clement do that?'

'Because Barclay was screwing his wife.'

I cast my mind back to the party, an event that was starting to seem like a long time ago. 'That'd be . . . Patty.'

'No, Tara, the one before Patty.'

'Jesus, d'you mean this whole thing's about a couple of rich bastards competing over models?'

'Yeah, and over money. They can scarcely tell the difference between sex and money. In my experience they get equally excited about both.'

Two things troubled me. I'd thought McGuinness had an active background of some kind, but the way he spoke suggested something else. If I was going to strike a deal with him I needed to size him up better.

'What's your history, Clive? How did you get involved with nasties like Greaves and Clement?'

'Why?'

'Just tell me. Your future depends on it.'

'I was a statistician. I worked with Barclay in the tax office. We were both into that Iron John shit back then. You know, weekend bivouacs and paint guns. Kids' stuff, but it gives you some moves and some sort of confidence, I suppose. Barclay persuaded me I could do better by working for him in the private sector. I have. Until now.'

'Okay, what about this? Greaves was at Clement's party a while back. He was putting shit on him, but how come he was there if there's so much bad blood between them?'

McGuinness drew the robe tighter around him for warmth and reassurance. 'You don't understand about these people, do you? They love to rub each other's noses in the dirt. You think mega-rich rivals don't invite each other to their big bashes? They do, all the time. They're polite on the surface and they fester underneath.'

What he was saying had a ring of truth to it, although I'd only glimpsed both protagonists briefly. McGuinness was acting like one of those Mafia informants who'd decided to spill all the beans and take his chances. In his case the risks weren't as great, but his involvement in Louise Kramer's death, whatever it was, had convinced him they were great enough.

'I believe you, Clive,' I said, 'and I'm prepared to let you drive the Beemer to Queensland or to Mascot with your passport in your pocket or whatever, but I need to know where Billie is.'

He nodded. 'I've got about a million frequent flyer points. I've got contacts in the States. I can make a living there.'

'What about this joint, and Dottie?'

He shrugged. 'Both rented. Dottie's not my wife. I don't know where the Marchant woman is, but I know who does know.'

'And who's that?'

'I need my guarantee.'

'So do I, that you tell me and then don't tell whoever it is that I'm on the way.'

'Why would I do that?'

'Because you're a slimy, slippery bastard and I can see the wheels turning in your head.'

We kicked it around for a while, with the evening grower cooler and McGuinness feeling it sharply in his wet state and needing a drink worse than I did. Eventually we came up with a solution: McGuinness booked a seat on a flight to Bangkok leaving in about three hours. I didn't allow him to shower and I watched him closely. He dressed in his tan lightweight suit, no tie, packed a bag and collected his passport. I'd drive him to the airport and stay with him all the way to the departure gate, keeping his boarding pass, ticket and passport in my pocket to that point. No phoning permitted. He agreed to tell me what I wanted to know when he was due to board. I told him that if what he said didn't check out I'd arrange for him to be arrested in Bangkok.

'Nasty gaols there, they tell me,' I said.

He looked sceptical. 'I don't think you'd have the clout. A crummy private eye.'

'Mate, all I'd have to do would be to say you were a terrorist, head of a cell here in Frenchs Forest with plans to set Ku-ring-gai Chase ablaze this summer. Drop a couple of cans of petrol in your garage with a few standard lighters. I've got your passport number and your flight details. They'd jump at it, the level of paranoia being what it is.'

'I suppose you're right.'

Give him his due, that was when he made his move and it was smart to do it after a reluctant compliance. I'd moved a little too close to him; he sensed it, got set, pivoted, and aimed a hard chop at my neck. We'd had another drink and he'd made his strong. Maybe the dousing in the pool had affected him. Either way, I saw the blow coming and swayed back in time. I shoved him hard while he was still moving and his hand cracked into the doorjamb. He let out a yell.

'That'll bruise,' I said. 'Might be broken.'

'Fuck you.'

'Never mind, those nice hosties on Thai Air'll look after you. Especially in business class.'

All the fight went out of him as he nursed his hand. He left the house without a backward glance, as if his life to that point was disposable. I took his wallet with his credit cards and his passport and put them in the door pocket on the driver's side of the car. He had to manage his suitcase with his left and he struggled to get it into the boot. Too bad. Another struggle to get buckled up and we were on our way.

We scarcely exchanged a word on the way to Mascot. McGuinness was slumped in his seat, obviously depressed and uncertain of his future. I was calculating the odds on his lying and leading me up a garden path or into something worse. I thought I had him bluffed, but it's a strategy you can never be sure of.

At the airport, I parked and he struggled to the check-in with his case and collected his ticket and boarding pass. I took them and his passport from him and we went to the bar.

We had almost an hour to wait and McGuinness got stuck into the scotch. I drank coffee. His right hand was changing colour but he could move and flex his fingers so it looked as though nothing was broken.

'Have them put some ice on it when you get on board,' I said.

He didn't reply. Bad loser.

He was about half drunk when his flight was called. I held his documents out of his reach, and bent towards him with my hand to my ear.

'Let's hear it, Clive.'

'How do I know you won't do what you said anyway?'

'You don't. You have to rely on my integrity. Come on, they're boarding.'

He let out a whisky-laden sigh. 'Rhys Thomas,' he said.

'What?'

'Rhys Thomas. D'you know him?'

'Yeah, I know him. He's Clement's muscle.'

The call came again and McGuinness stood. 'They handed Marchant over to Thomas.'

'Who's they?'

'Phil Courtney, the guy I was with in your shitty motel room and a nurse—well, she would've looked like a nurse.'

'I don't get it, Thomas works for Clement.'

'Clement thinks he does, but he's really Barclay's man. He's got an interest in a sort of physiotherapy clinic in Manly. I suppose that's where she is.'

'What's it called?'

'I don't know. I told you I could only give you a name. I don't know what it's called. Just that it's in Manly somewhere. Thomas is going to get the information, whatever it is, and use it against Clement for Barclay. Now give me the fucking ticket.'

It sounded plausible, something unlikely to be invented on the spur of the moment by a stressed, frightened man. His flight had been called; now he was being paged and he hadn't passed through customs. We moved towards the area and an impatient-looking attendant beckoned us. It looked as if the tardy passenger would be escorted through and rushed to the plane. That should prevent any phoning. I handed over the documents; he almost fell into the arms of the attendant.

There were three physiotherapy clinics listed for Manly in the phone book. I wrote down their names, called in at the first Internet café I saw and checked on them. One place, North Steyne Physio and Orthopaedics, announced a speciality in injuries and discomforts associated with horse riding. Had to be the one, given Thomas's racing background. I was low on petrol after covering so much of Sydney; I stopped to fill up the tank and myself. I bought a kebab, a stubby of stout and a takeaway coffee with sugar—nothing like a diversity of cultures food and drink-wise—and consumed them in the car while I considered what to do next.

If Billie Marchant was at the Manly clinic, there were bound to be people guarding her. If she wasn't, there was a good chance she was dead. As I ate and drank I pondered what the information she had could possibly be. Lou Kramer had given me no inkling other than that she thought it could be important—something to do with what had got Eddie killed, perhaps about someone ill-disposed towards Clement within his organisation. Subsequent events tended to confirm that but had brought no enlightenment.

The first thing to do was take a look at the clinic. I drove to Manly and located it a block away from North Steyne, close to Pittwater Road. The photo on the web page had flattered it. It was a nondescript two storey building in the middle of a set of three. The one to the left was a secondhand bookstore and the one on the right was up for lease. I went around the block and drove past it twice.

Manly being Manly, there was a fairly constant flow of traffic and no convenient parking places. I found one a block away and came back on foot to do a recce. There were lights on in the upper level of the building housing the clinic but its street-front windows and door were dark.

I kept on the other side of the one-way street, walked down to the next crossroad, and circled around to try to get a look at the back. A laneway ran behind the buildings fronting the road and I walked up it until I was standing facing a high brick wall with the clinic behind it, its upper level lights muted but visible. The gate in the wall looked impregnable, but the rickety fence of the place up for lease next door offered possibilities.

Still, no obvious strategy presented itself, not for a one-man operation. I needed support. I reached for my mobile, and swore. Disliking the thing, I'd left it in the car, a bad habit I was having trouble breaking. I walked back to the car and put the key in the lock. I felt a blow to my back and pitched forward against the car. Something cold and metallic jabbed me twice behind the ear and then I could smell it rather than feel it. He kept me pressed against the car door.

'Well, well, if it isn't Mr Nuisance himself. Cannot learn a lesson.'

South African accent, youngish voice. At a guess, Jonas Clement Junior.

'You can't shoot me here,' I said.

'This is silenced, Mr Hardy. You would just be another collapsing drunk being helped by a big, strong young fellow like me. You'll cross the road and go into the place you were so curious about. Very careless is what you are, man.'

17

You don't argue with a big ex-mercenary holding a silenced gun, but you muster what dignity and weapons you can. I relaxed under his pressure and quietly pocketed the keys.

'Okay,' I said. 'You're holding the cards, Jonas.'

He clipped my ear, quickly and stingingly, with the pistol and then eased back. 'That's for being cheeky. Now we wait for a break in the traffic and go across. Straight across. If you run or go left or right, you're dead.'

I stepped back from the car and he shepherded me around it to face the road. The traffic wasn't heavy and he prodded me forward.

'You've done this before,' I said.

'You just bet I have, and enjoyed it, too.'

'Yeah, in Africa. Probably with twelve-year-olds, fourteen tops, old women maybe.'

'You're talking yourself into your grave.'

We were across the road. The darkened door slid open and I went through into a carpeted area, lit only by the torch a big man was carrying.

'Him again,' he said, and I knew he was another of my Toxteth hotel friends.

'Yes, Kezza, him again. I thought so.'

'How did he . . . ?'

'He's going to tell us. You rang Rhys?'

'He's on his way.'

'Right. So, we'll find somewhere to make Mr fucking Hardy uncomfortable while we wait. See if he's carrying anything of interest.'

Kezza slapped my pockets and took the keys. 'Where's your wallet?'

It was in the glove box with the .38 and I didn't want them looking. For ease of access, I'd put a few things in my shirt pocket earlier—my investigator's licence, some cash and a credit card. I tapped the pocket. 'Don't carry one.'

Kezza took the licence, the card and the money. Clement turned on a light and we went up the stairs to where a series of rooms ran off a narrow passage. He pushed me into a room and slammed and locked the door. The room was small; it had no window and contained only a lightly padded massage or treatment bench without any covering and a locked cabinet that presumably contained items to do with physiotherapy. I sat on the bench and leaned back against the wall. Clement had been right—driving past the place slowly twice, parking too close and not being careful around the back had been sloppy work.

I'd expected some pretty heavy security inside if Billie was being held here, but why the close watch on what came and went outside? I hadn't anticipated that and found it puzzling. What were they expecting? I knew McGuinness hadn't alerted them and I couldn't come up with any explanation. I gave up and concentrated on trying to gain some sort of advantage. The cabinet was solid and firmly locked. The door likewise. The walls and ceiling were smooth plasterboard; the overhead light was covered by a screwed-down plastic shield. The lino tiles on the floor were tightly glued into place. I had my fists and feet, nothing else. Maybe my brains.

I stretched out on the bench and tried to remember exactly what McGuinness had said about Rhys Thomas. *He's really Barclay's man.* Assuming Kezza and Clement weren't aware of this, and there was no other heavy in the place, that could be my advantage.

After about an hour, multiple footsteps sounded in the passage and the door was unlocked. Rhys Thomas came in accompanied by Clement. I stayed where I was.

'You look relaxed, Hardy,' Thomas said.

'I've been in worse places.'

'I'll bet you have. So have I, so has Jonas here. How's the eye?'

'Just a split in old scar tissue. It wasn't as bad as it looked.'

'You were a fighter, were you?'

'Among other things. Is Wilhelmina here?'

'Who?'

I sat up. 'Thought you mightn't know. That's her name. Billie's short for Wilhelmina.'

'This man is a real smartarse, Rhys,' Clement said. 'I vote we take him to the Gap and push him off.'

'Not very original,' I said.

Clement took two steps forward with two fists clenched. 'You make me angry, man.'

'Short fuse. Insecure. Probably something to do with your father.'

'Stop it, Hardy,' Thomas said. 'Your pop psychology's a load of shit. Jonas here just loves violence, goes well with his bad temper.'

'Don't talk about me as if I'm not here,' Clement said.

Thomas looked at him. 'It might be best for you not to have been here, Jonas. Depends on how things turn out.'

Clement shrugged, retreated and seemed to lose interest, leaning back against the wall.

That remark reminded me of Thomas's quick response when I'd kidded him about Dylan Thomas. He wasn't the thug he sometimes appeared. It also made me suspect what McGuinness had said about him being Barclay's man was right. He was slightly bow-legged, partly disguised by loose black trousers, but solidly built. He wore a cream linen shirt and boots with a bit of heel. Lifted him to maybe 180 centimetres. Touch of vanity there. As on party night, his thinning brown hair was slicked straight back. At a guess his teeth were false; probably hit a rail or got hit by a hoof somewhere along the line.

'The woman's here, Hardy,' Thomas said. 'But how did you find out?'

I shook my head. 'Sworn to secrecy.'

An impatient grunt from Clement, ignored by Thomas.

'Doesn't matter. But we've got a problem. I bet you'd like a drink.'

Was this Thomas showing his hand? Didn't seem likely with Clement looming there in the background, but anything to get out of this room which was starting to feel airless and to smell a bit.

'Sure,' I said.

Thomas inclined his head. We went out and down the passage with Thomas leading and Clement following close behind at my shoulder. I picked up the source of the smell—Jonas Clement Junior had very bad BO.

At the end of the passage there was a sitting area with lounge chairs and a low table. A sort of down-market conference room. I dropped into one of the chairs, grateful for the comfort after the hard bench. Clement, looking bored, sat not far from me. I gave a couple of puzzled sniffs in his direction; he scowled at me, opened his jacket and let me see the holstered pistol.

Thomas put my keys, cards and money on the table as items of no interest. Bad sign. He opened a bar fridge, took out a can of beer and tossed it roughly in Clement's direction. He stretched out a long arm and caught it easily—nothing wrong with the reactions.

'What d'you fancy, Hardy?' Thomas said.

But I didn't really know what he was up to and I wasn't going to play good-guy games with him. 'It doesn't fucking matter, Rhys. Whatever you like. Let's get on with it.'

Thomas poured two solid slugs of vodka and dropped in a few ice cubes. He handed me a glass and bared his too-white and even teeth in a smile. 'We've got a problem with Ms Marchant. She won't respond in any way. We think she's faking but how can you tell with a zonked-out junkie like that?'

I drank some of the icy vodka and felt it warm and encourage me the way it should. 'My heart bleeds for you. Maybe she's suffered brain damage from being buggered about by you and your goons.'

Thomas shook his head. 'I don't think so and neither does a doctor we brought in to look at her. Pulse fine, blood pressure okay, etc.'

Clement had sucked down his beer in no time flat. He

crushed the can in his fist. 'Fuck this. Let's work this prick over until he tells us how he got here and then let me have a go at the woman. In Africa we worked out certain things about women—what they really didn't like, you know?'

Thomas had a long pull on his drink and shrugged. 'You see how things stand, Hardy? Jonas here is impatient and wants to use his considerable experience.'

'The impetuosity of youth,' I said.

'Fuck you,' Clement said. 'Give me another beer, Rhys, and I'll show you some of the things you can do with an empty can.'

Thomas said, 'Jonas isn't subtle, is he? Scary though.'

'One-on-one I'd give myself a chance,' I said. 'Fifty-fifty, I'd say. But like all bullying cowards that wouldn't be his style.'

Thomas tossed off the rest of his drink. 'This is all bullshit. I'm in charge here and I've got a different idea. Marchant won't talk to us, but I think she would to your girlfriend.'

I looked and felt blank.

'Ms Sharon Marchant. You're going to get her here to persuade her sister to be sensible.'

I almost laughed. 'You're dreaming. She's not my girlfriend.'

'Really? You disappoint me. Doesn't matter. We need her here and you're going to get her to come.'

'I don't think so.'

'Do you know a Sarah Marchant-Wallambi? Bloody silly name but there you are.'

I didn't respond.

'I can tell that you do. Well, when I heard about you being here, I arranged to have a colleague stationed outside her flat in Campbelltown. I'm told that a young man by the name of Craig Williamson has just left in his Mercedes sports—God knows how these youngsters get the money—and she's there alone. Her flatmate, one Jenny Timms, a fellow student at the university, is out. My colleague wouldn't have any trouble getting Ms Marchant-Wallambi under his control. D'you want any more? Like the address, or the registration number of her mum's VW? Perhaps you'd prefer my bloke to get her on the phone, just to be sure?'

'No. I believe you. Low-life of your sort just love taking advantage of women.'

'That's the truth, us not being white knights like you, although I suspect you're just a bit grey at times. Right?'

'You wouldn't have a clue.'

He ignored that, detached a mobile from his belt and checked its charge. 'What's her number, Jonas?'

Clement, still not happy, took a notebook from his pocket and read the number off. Thomas tossed me the phone. 'Make it convincing.'

I punched in the numbers and Sharon came on the line.

'Sharon, it's Hardy. I've . . . located Billie.'

'That's great. Where is she?'

'Manly.'

'Manly! What the hell's she doing there. Is she in a hospital or what?'

'Look, Sharon, there's no easy way to do this. The people who took her are still in control. We're not out of the woods. They want you to come here and try to persuade her to tell them what she knows.'

'What kind of shit is this? I thought you said—'

'Listen, these are serious people, very serious, and apparently there's a lot at stake. You have to come.'

'I don't have to do anything. Are you in with them? I'm not going to make her talk to a bunch of kidnappers.'

'Sharon, they've got someone at Sarah's flat. She's on her own.'

Clement was making a call on his phone. He gestured to me to let Sharon hear what he was saying in a loud voice with his accent at full, menacing strength. 'That is right. If you hear the phone ring anytime in the next couple of minutes, go right in and grab her.'

So Clement wasn't dumb either. I heard a shout of anger from Sharon. Thomas took the phone from me. 'Ms Marchant, if you do as we ask your daughter won't be disturbed. She won't even know what happened. You can ring her when you get here and tell her to get Craig over there, if you wish. Until then my man is standing by.'

Thomas returned the phone to me. 'They're calling the shots,' I said. 'I think they're telling the truth about Sarah. They know the address, Craig's car, all that.'

'God, this is a nightmare. What do they *want*?'

'I wish I knew.'

'All right. I'll come. Where is it?'

I told her; Thomas snatched the phone and cut the connection.

I finished the drink and put the glass on the table. 'How about letting me see Billie? I knew Eddie Flannery pretty well and he's supposed to be the source of whatever it is you're trying to find out. She just might talk to me if I tell a story or two about Eddie.'

Clement shook his head and yawned but Thomas thought it over and nodded. 'Why not?'

I gathered up my things. Clement moved to stop me, but Thomas, still unconcerned, waved him off. We went downstairs to a room at the back of the building. While it wasn't exactly medical in atmosphere, it wasn't like a bedroom either. The bed was metal framed and the furniture in the room was functional. The washbasin in the corner, though, gave it a slightly sleazy feel. A woman lay on the bed covered by a sheet and a blanket. Her eyes were closed. I went closer and could see the dark roots starting to get more prominent against the blonde hair. She was pale but with that slight tint to her skin like Sharon. In facial features they were much alike, but this woman had been through a lot more of life's hoops.

I looked at Thomas. 'You said all her vital signs . . . whatever you call them are okay?'

'Check 'em if you like.'

'I wouldn't know how.'

'I do,' Clement said. He put two fingers on her wrist. 'Pulse a bit slow but not much.' He picked up a device from the table by the bed, placed it near her ear and clicked. 'Temperature up just a bit.' He lifted one eyelid in a surprisingly delicate movement. 'Nothing wrong. The bitch is faking.'

'Billie,' I said, 'I knew your bloke Eddie pretty well when he was in the PEA game. Worked with him once or twice. I remember when he fucked the wife of that copper who was giving him trouble. What was her name again? Ruby, that's it, Ruby Collins.'

Clement yawned again. 'Nothing.'

'She twitched,' I said.

Clement flicked a cigarette lighter. 'She'd do more than twitch if I had my way.'

Billie lay as still as a statue.

'We'll see what the sister can do,' Thomas said.

18

They put me back in the windowless room after allowing me to take a piss. I was weary and fell asleep on the hard bench, pillow or no pillow. I was awake when the door opened and Clement beckoned me out. 'She's here. Looks more human than her sister.'

'What would you know about humanity?'

'Keep it up, Hardy.'

He herded me back to the sick room where Thomas was standing on one side of the bed with Sharon on the other. The look she gave me would have cut glass.

'I'm sorry,' I said. 'Did you phone Sarah?'

'Yes,' she said, not looking at me. 'Craig's on his way.'

Thomas rubbed the grey bristles on his face. It'd been a long day for all of us, him included. 'Let's get on with it, Ms Marchant. See if you can get a response from her.'

'Is she sedated?' Sharon asked.

'She was, mildly. It must have worn off by now. My colleague here has some medical knowledge and believes she's faking. He's in favour of . . . sterner measures.'

'Torture,' I said.

'Shut up, Hardy,' Thomas snapped. 'You're not helping. The sooner we find out what we need to know the sooner everyone can go home or into hospital or do whatever the hell they want. With certain exceptions.'

Sharon leaned closer to her inert sister. 'She's very thin in the face, gaunt. She looks dehydrated. She was deep in malnutrition . . .'

'They put her on drips in the hospital and treated the pneumonia with antibiotics,' Thomas said. 'She's functional. Get through to her, lady. Convince her that the best course is for her to talk to us.'

Sharon shook her head. 'She's a burnt-out case. Maybe the best course is for her to die here peacefully and for all you bastards to just fuck off.'

'Sharon?' Billie said.

Thomas smiled. 'Good work.'

'Not for you, bandy legs,' Sharon snarled. 'Billie, babe, we've really got ourselves in the shit here.'

'I know,' Billie said. 'I was hoping they'd just give me a shot of something eventually and let me just . . .'

'You're finished with shots of something. I've got twenty grand to put you in detox, rehab, whatever, and get you back on your feet. Come on, babe, there's Sammy to consider, and me and Sarah.'

'Sammy,' Billie whispered. 'Is he okay?'

Sharon smoothed sweat-stiffened hair from Billie's face. 'Yeah, he is. But these people've got a long reach. They threatened Sarah.'

Billie made an effort and hoisted herself up a little so that she wasn't just lying flat on the bed. Sharon adjusted the pillow behind her. 'Jesus,' Billie said, 'I don't know what's going on. It's been a blur for a while and, fuck, I could do with a fix now.'

'No chance,' Clement said.

Thomas looked as though he wanted to hit him. 'Just possibly,' he said.

Sharon shrugged and murmured in tune—' "The kids are all right". Remember that? It applies now. Maybe we should just tell these bastards to get fucked. We've provided the next generation. What's so great about life right now?'

Clement pushed me aside and moved closer to the bed. 'Listen, you cunt. I can give you so much pain you'll tell me where this Sammy is and plead for me to kill him rather than go on doing what I'm doing to you.'

'He's capable of it, believe me,' Thomas said.

The colour drained from Sharon's face but she stood her ground. She turned away from Clement and addressed Thomas: 'I'm not going to do a thing while that animal's in the room. Get rid of him and I'll talk to her.'

Clement protested but Thomas overruled him and ordered him out. As soon as the door closed with a well-sealed hiss, Thomas took out a pistol, waved me to a corner of the room and spoke urgently. 'He's very dangerous.'

'Who's to say you won't just kill us if you get what you want?' Sharon said. 'And what if Billie doesn't know anything?'

'I know plenty,' Billie said. 'You sure about that twenty grand, sis?'

'I've got it,' Sharon said.

Billie turned, propped herself on an elbow, and looked at me. 'Is he any fucking use?'

Good question. 'Listen, Rhys,' I said. 'I know you're working for Greaves, not Clement.'

The look on Thomas's face told me that I was right on the money. His secret was out; he was in danger and he knew it. The question was how would he react? He could probably afford to kill me, but not Sharon and Billie. He must have been playing a cagey game between Clement and Greaves for some time but he hadn't anticipated this and it threw him. I had to move quickly to make the most of the advantage.

'Clive McGuinness told me when I put him under some pressure,' I said. 'But he's out of the picture now, on his way to Bangkok.'

'Fucking McGuinness,' Thomas said. 'That's how you got here.'

'Yeah, that's right.'

Billie's cigarette and booze eroded voice cut in: 'Who—?'

'Shut up.' I pointed to the door and got Thomas's attention. 'Young Clement's nuts, you can see that. You've barely got him under control. Get what you want from Billie and I'll help you take care of him. Then you can play it your way with Greaves and we're out of here and we've never heard of you.'

It wasn't ideal, with everything coming down to Billie. From what I'd heard of her, and given her state of health, there was no way to tell which way she'd jump. She'd showed some spirit, but now she was looking dubiously at all three of us about equally. She had no way to know whether to trust Thomas or me and I could sense the history of conflict between the two sisters. She closed her eyes and Sharon grabbed her by the shoulders and shook her.

'Billie, you can't flake out now.'

'What about something to get me up and running?'

'Maybe,' Thomas said, looming over her. 'But let's make this quick. Hardy's right about Jonas. He's dangerous. He hates me, hates his old man, hates everybody and particularly women who give him a bad time. Here's what I want to know. It's likely what got Eddie killed. Don't you make the same mistake. Where's Peter Scriven?'

19

So that's what it was all about—Peter Scriven and his missing millions. If McGuinness was right, Clement knew where he was and was blackmailing him and Greaves wanted in on the action. On that analysis, it looked as if Clement Junior was being kept in the dark by his dad and planned to change things in his favour. Poor Clement Senior, betrayed on all sides. 'It's always about the money' someone said, and they were just about right.

I was absorbing this when the door swung in and Jonas Clement came barging through.

'I've had enough of this shit. What's she saying . . . ?'

Thomas took a pistol from his pocket and shot Clement twice in the chest at close range. I was never going to get a better chance. I took three long strides and hit Thomas with a haymaker right that caught him on the hinge of his jaw. It had all my weight and forward movement behind it; bones grated and separated and skin split as he sagged, dropped his gun and collapsed in a heap.

Sharon was standing stock still, and Billie had fallen back on the bed. I shook Sharon hard. 'Pick her up. She's just skin and bone. You can carry her. We're getting out of here.'

'Is he . . . dead?'

'Yes. Move!'

Thomas had cracked the back of his head on the floor and was unconscious. I bent over Clement, avoided the blood soaking his shirt and flipped open his jacket. The silenced gun slid out of the holster smooth as a snake. Then I picked up Thomas's pistol. Sharon shook her head, wiggled fingers in her ears to clear them after the loud reports in the confined space, and grabbed a rigid Billie under the armpits. She raised her easily and slung her over her shoulder in a fireman's lift, taking a sheet with her. She got her balance and looked at me.

The door stood open and I heard movement outside. Kezza, with a piece of metal piping in his hand, was moving cautiously down the passage. I stepped out and pointed Clement's gun at him.

'Down. Right down. Drop the pipe and don't move a muscle.'

He kept coming and I fired, aiming at the ceiling just over his head. The pistol made a muted pop but a detached chunk of plasterboard showered him.

'It's Jonas's quiet gun, Kezza. But I think it's pretty effective. Want to see?'

He dropped the pipe and stood there.

'Down!'

He lay flat on the floor, face down.

'Good. Jonas is dead and Rhys is out of action. What you do next is up to you, but I'm leaving with the women and you don't stir until we're gone. Agreed?'

He nodded, hitting his chin and swearing.

I leaned back into the room and waved Sharon forward. 'We're off. Put Billie in your car and follow me.'

'Where're we going?'

'I'll think of somewhere.'

The traffic had slowed and there was no sign that Thomas's shots had attracted any attention. Kezza certainly wouldn't be calling the cops. Sharon's car was parked ahead of mine and I helped her to load an unresisting Billie onto the back seat. I got to my car and drove past her, moving slowly until I was sure she'd picked me up. I'd shoved both pistols inside my shirt where they sat, cold and slick with sweat, sticky with blood, above my belt. I drove without any thought of a direction while I turned things over in my mind. Who would Kezza contact? Depended what side he was really on and there was no way of telling that, but the odds were he'd get to Clement Senior first to tell him about the death of his son. He'd know from the wounds I hadn't used his son's small-calibre silenced gun and that the killer had to be Thomas, but would he and whoever came to help leave it that way?

And what of Thomas? He could claim I'd flattened him, taken his gun and used it on Clement. That's if he could talk. It'd be a thin story but Thomas was smart, smarter than Kezza, that was for sure.

Sharon, almost tailgating, flashed her high beam lights at me, worried about where we were heading. I needed somewhere safe to go to think through this maze. It came to me as I had to decide to turn towards the city or go north. I made the decision, took the turn and raised a fist in a determined gesture to indicate a purpose.

Sharon got the message and dropped back to a comfortable position.

Clement knew where I lived and worked and so, no doubt, did Barclay Greaves. Greaves also knew where Sharon lived and about Billie's sojourn in Liston. I used to have a good bolt-hole in the Rooftop Motel in Glebe where they'd let me put my car out of sight and didn't bother about registering me. But the Rooftop was up for redevelopment and was closed. Always best to stick as close as you can to your own turf. I drove on automatic pilot until I pulled up outside Mike D'Angelo's projected Lilyfield dream home. A single light showed inside. Tommy was doing the right thing, minding the store.

I told Sharon to wait in the car. I put the guns under the driver's seat, handling them carefully, and went through the gate that opened easily now that it wasn't weed-entangled. There was a strong, pleasant smell of slashed fennel and the cat-piss stink of cut lantana in the yard. I went to the front door and knocked quietly. The door opened cautiously.

'Hey, Tommy.'

'Cliff, my man. Watcha doin' here?'

'A bit of trouble, mate. I need a place to lie low for a day or so. Me and two women.'

'*Two* women. Wow! I could do with one.'

'Not like that. Okay by you?'

'Sure, there's plenty of space and I've cleaned the place up a bit. Not real comfortable, but.'

'Doesn't matter. Thanks, Tommy. I'll get them.'

We helped Billie from the car. She was weak but she wanted to walk and managed it with some support, although Sharon practically had to lift her up the steps.

Tommy had turned on a few lights and we went into the wide hallway typical of the best Federation houses.

'She sick?' Tommy asked.

'Yeah,' I said, 'but getting better. Is there a bed?'

'Sort of, a sofa, like.'

I explained to Sharon about Tommy's job and how he'd been useful to me out at Liston. She helped Billie onto a sofa in the room Tommy showed us. It was big; polished board floor, high ceiling and double doors standing open led through to the kitchen. I could see that he'd swept the floors and wiped the surfaces. Cobwebs hung thickly in the corners of the rooms.

'I eat in the kitchen or out on the back porch. There's four bedrooms with ratty mattresses. I've only cleaned one out.'

'We'll manage. Anything to drink?'

'Tea, coffee, coke.'

'Nothing stronger?'

He shook his head.

'I've got some brandy in the car,' Sharon said. 'I thought it might be needed.'

'It is,' I said. 'Tommy, is there any way I can get my car out of sight?'

He pointed to the dirt and stains on his once-white overalls. 'I cleared all the shit away that was blocking the gate to the drive this arvo. Fuckin' hard work, too. You can put it in there. Out of sight from the street.'

Sharon, squatting by the sofa, and Billie were talking quietly.

'How is she?' I said.

'Not bad. Coming down from the sedation. I'm a bit worried about how she'll be when she hits bottom.'

'I've got a doctor friend who'll give her something but probably not till morning.'

Billie mumbled something and Sharon shook her head. 'She could be bad by then.'

'I've got some Panadol somewhere,' I said. 'Might knock her out with the brandy.'

'She a junkie?' Tommy asked.

'Sort of,' Sharon said. 'Yeah, she's been getting treatment but she's had a shock tonight. We all have.'

Crouched as she was there in the half-light, Sharon's profile in shadow on the wall was slightly different with a hint of Aboriginality in her features.

'I've got a little bit of grass,' Tommy said. 'For emergencies. Hey, you a sister?'

'Back a bit. Thinned out by now.'

'Doesn't matter. You're welcome to the dope if you need it.'

'Thanks. And she's my sister by the way.'

Tommy let go with one of his grins. 'Hey, Cliff, you're the odd one out here.'

'Wouldn't be the first time.'

I took Sharon's keys and went outside to move the Falcon and get the brandy. There was no moon and the street lights barely reached the yard, but the wide gate came open without too much effort and I parked the car where a couple of tall she-oaks would give it some cover. The bottle of Rémy Martin was almost full and I took a good swig before I went back into the house. It's not every night you deal with an abduction, plus a murder and go into hiding from two powerful enemies. I took another swig.

For all his brutality, Jonas Clement Junior had seemed to know what he was about when he checked Billie's vital signs. She was pale and shaky, still wearing a faded nightdress Sharon had brought for her in hospital, but she wolfed down a peanut butter sandwich made by Tommy, drank a cup of milky instant coffee heavily laced with brandy, took a couple of Panadol and was ready to call it a night. We bedded her down on the sofa with Sharon's jacket for a pillow, the sheet from the clinic, and an old rug from my car as extra cover because she was shivering slightly. She was snoring within minutes, but her breathing was shallow.

'I've gotta go to bed, guys,' Tommy announced. 'I start as soon as the sun's up. I'll try not to disturb youse.'

We thanked him and he left, padding barefoot down the hallway. Sharon settled herself in the only chair in the room, an old padded number leaking horsehair. 'I'm sleeping here.'

'Right,' I said. 'I'll see if I can find a sheet or something for you.'

I turned on the lights in the rooms Tommy hadn't dealt with other than replacing globes, and had to breathe shallowly against the smell of dead insects and stale air. Both rooms had a couple of mattresses, one on top of another, covered with thin grey blankets. When I shook out the blankets the rooms filled with dust and the blankets turned out to have been less grey originally. I took one through to Sharon who sniffed at it and sneezed.

'If I get cold,' she said. 'Right, Cliff, I guess we're safe here for now, but tell me what's going on.'

I laid it all out, as much to get it clear in my own mind as for her benefit. How Clement knew the whereabouts of Peter Scriven, the financier who'd absconded with multimillions, how Barclay Greaves wanted to horn in on the blackmail and settle an old score with Clement. I knew that

Rhys Thomas, while on Clement's payroll, was actually working for Greaves and I guessed that Clement Junior was either tied in with Thomas or planning to go it alone, probably the latter.

'And all over what my junkie sister might or might not know?'

'Yeah. Eddie Flannery found out something he shouldn't, probably where Scriven is and what name he's going under and so on. Clement had him killed but they think he passed the information on to Billie.'

'What about your ex-client, Kramer?'

'Hard to say. She was being helped in her research into Clement by Greaves, but whether she knew what his real intention was I don't know. Somehow she got in the way and ended up dead.'

'Who did that?'

'At a guess a guy named Phil Courtney who works for Greaves.'

'But why?'

'You met her. She was a hard case. Maybe Greaves told her he didn't need her anymore after he thought he'd got control of Billie. Maybe she threatened him. Maybe she had something on him.'

'Like what?'

I shrugged. 'Who knows? Maybe he had Eddie killed, not Clement, and Lou knew about it.'

'Was she that hard a case?'

'She was pretty desperate. But, look, it all comes back to Billie—what she knows.'

The night had cooled down and Sharon pulled the dusty blanket close and tucked her legs up under it. The room had a fireplace and would be a nice, cosy spot in winter with a few logs burning. Sharon handed me her empty coffee cup and I poured her some brandy.

'If anything,' she said.

'How'd you mean? She said she knew plenty.'

Sharon sipped the brandy and let out a long sigh. 'The chips were down, or that's how it looked, and when the chips were down Billie'd always do the same thing—lie.'

Billie was on the sofa not far away and still emitting tiny snores. But then, she'd faked a kind of coma for a long time back in Manly. I glanced at her and Sharon followed the look.

'That's right,' she said. 'D'you know what David Niven said about Errol Flynn?'

'Remind me.'

'He said, "You could rely on Errol. He'd always let you down." That's our Billie.'

'Terrific.'

'Why? Were you hoping she'd tell you where this rich runaway is so you could grab some glory? Sorry, Cliff, sorry, that's unfair after all you've done. It's just that it's been a hell of a day, with guns going off and Sarah under threat and this old spooky house and everything.'

'It's okay, Sharon. But we've got two ruthless rich bastards to contend with and maybe the cops as well, depending on how Clement and Greaves play it. So I was hoping that we could use what Billie knows to get us out of this jam.'

She drained her cup. 'Well, we'll just have to wait, won't we? I'm going to try to get some sleep, but leave the light on, okay?'

20

Whatever the old mattresses were filled with, mine had set hard and lumpy. Sharon had taken the right option. I stripped, used my clothes as a pillow, and stretched out anyway with the dusty blanket over me, and all the guns to hand. I didn't expect to sleep with so many questions begging for answers inside my brain, but I did, fitfully. I woke up with light streaming through the many missing slats of a venetian blind. True to his word, Tommy was at work already, slashing and raking. It was close to 7 am with the sun well up.

Somehow I'd found, or engineered with my tossing and turning, a more or less comfortable niche in the decrepit mattress. I lay there, dozing on my back, until a fit of sneezing brought on by the dust in the blanket and the room forced me to get up. As I stood there, I had to laugh. I'd hated the discipline in the army and the routine in the insurance company work, but those jobs didn't involve standing around in my briefs with my nose streaming and blood-smeared guns on the floor. Say what you like about the kind of work you're in now, Cliff, I thought, but at least it's not predictable.

I looked in on the two sisters and both were asleep in a room kept dark by heavy curtains and with the doors to the kitchen closed. The light bulb had blown. In the bathroom I found a few scraps of soap and two old towels. I showered, dried off, took the damp towel out to the back porch and hung it over a rail. Tommy saw me and raised his hand but didn't stop working. I fetched my travelling kit—razor, lather stick, toothbrush and comb—from the car, shaved and tidied myself up. I made a cup of instant coffee, thought about the brandy but decided against it. As I put the bottle down Sharon appeared in the doorway.

'Do you usually drink with your morning coffee?'

'It's been known.'

'Does it help?'

'Seems to, sometimes.'

'Well, go ahead.'

'I don't think so. Make you a coffee?'

'A latte.'

'Funny.'

She ran her hands through her hair and did some stretching exercises that made me feel stiff just to watch. I brewed the coffee and put the mug on the table.

'Thanks. It's not funny though, is it, Cliff? What're we going to do?'

I sipped the hot coffee and wished I had spiked it. 'How's Billie?'

'Still out. You haven't answered my question.'

'First thing is to get my doctor mate over to take a look at her.'

'Then?'

'Give me break, Sharon. I've never had to deal with anything quite like this before.'

One of the first things I'd done after being hired by Lou Kramer was to take a note of the time slot of Jonas Clement's radio program. I hadn't got around to listening to it, but now I tuned in to the FM station on the Falcon's radio: *Owing to unforeseen circumstances, Jonas Clement will not be heard in his 'You talk, we listen' slot today. Bruce Salter will stand in for him.*

So Clement knew about his son's death, but I was willing to bet there'd be nothing about it in the papers. Clement would have to contrive some kind of story and invent the circumstances to make it convincing. Big ask, but he had the connections to pull it off.

I phoned Ian Sangster and he arrived soon after. Ian's been my doctor since I got to Glebe and he's stitched me up and medicated me more times than I can count. He's a drinker and smoker who says his goal in life is to prove medical correctness about alcohol and nicotine and exercise is all wrong. So far, he's holding his own. I introduced him to Sharon and we went in to where Billie was stirring. Ian has dealt with me in various places other than his surgery and nothing about the Lilyfield set-up fazed him.

'Change not to be patching you up, mate,' he said.

Sharon introduced him to Billie and gave an account of what she'd been through recently. Billie was decidedly shaky, trembling and sweating. Ian waved me out of the room and it was some time before he called me back. He has a good manner and she had apparently let him examine her thoroughly. He stood up, felt for his cigarettes and lighter. Billie stretched out her hand for one but he shook his head.

'Not now, Ms Marchant. Sorry, but you've got an upper respiratory tract infection. We need to get some antibiotics into you to clear your lungs. Then you can puff away as I do.'

'What else?' Sharon said.

Ian fiddled with the cigarette. One of his techniques is to talk to the patient directly, not to go through intermediaries. 'At a guess,' he said to Billie, 'you've got some serious dependency problems, plus you're underweight and, I'd be willing to bet, constipated.'

Billie nodded. Her voice had a wheeze and a raw, Marianne Faithfull quality. 'Spot on, Doc.'

'So?' Sharon said.

Ian looked around the room; the blanket over the chair Sharon had slept in, Sharon and me both in unwashed clothes, the air of a place far from functional.

'Tight spot, Cliff?'

'You could say that.'

He spoke to Billie again. 'You require proper medication and nursing, agreed?'

Billie sank back against Sharon's jacket. She didn't need to say anything. She closed her eyes and we could hear her heavy, laboured breathing. Ian pulled the rug up to her chin and patted her head. 'You'll be okay.'

He drew Sharon and me away to the kitchen and requested a cup of coffee. He saw the brandy bottle and held it up to the light. 'Spike it, Cliff.'

I made the coffee and he sipped it appreciatively. 'Your sister should be in hospital, Sharon, but I gather that's not an option.'

'No,' I said. 'Some high-powered people will be checking precisely that.'

Ian lit the cigarette, drew deeply and sipped the coffee. 'Okay. I'll leave you some Valium and I can arrange for a nurse to come here and give her the antibiotics and ventolin and monitor her progress for forty-eight hours. That's the best I can do. If she's not significantly improved by then she goes to hospital whatever the consequences. Cliff, you know I'm putting my licence on the line here.'

'Thanks, Ian.'

'Thank you, doctor,' Sharon said.

'I'll bill you, Cliff. Big time.'

'I can pay,' Sharon said.

I waved away Ian's smoke. 'He's joking, Sharon. We work it out in bottles of red.'

'Blokes,' Sharon said.

Ian left and I went out to see how Tommy was getting on and to do some thinking. He'd cleared most of the lantana and other vines and was working on a corner of the yard choked by some shrub with multiple stems and stalks that looked ready to take over the world. He stopped and wiped away sweat.

'You're doing a great job.'

'Thanks. It's harder than I thought but I'm getting there.'

'Mike been round?'

'Once. He seemed happy.'

'Should be. Sorry about barging in like this. Couldn't think of anywhere else to go.'

'Cops after you?'

'Could be, but they're not the main worry. We won't be here long.'

'Not a problem. How's the sickie?'

'Not too good, that's why we'll have to move soon. Found anything interesting under all the crap, apart from the statues?'

'Mostly bottles, man, mostly bottles.'

I hadn't thought about the police for a while and I began to consider them as the best option despite Sharon's earlier objections. Things had got more serious since then. I went back into the house to find Billie sitting up and nursing a big glass of brandy. Two pills lay on the rug.

'She won't take the Valium,' Sharon said. 'Reckons she's all right. I've been thinking. Looks to me as if we'll have to go to the police and tell them the whole story.'

'No,' Billie yelled and then collapsed with a fit of coughing. She hung on to the brandy though.

Sharon tried to put her arm around her but Billie shook her off. 'Look, Billie, I know there's warrants and stuff on you but we can work it out. Cliff'll help, won't you?'

I nodded but I could see Billie wasn't buying it. She fought for breath and took a big drink when she was able. 'I can't have anything to do with the cops.'

'Why?' Sharon said.

'I can't tell you.'

'Jesus, after all I've—'

Billie could only get a few words out at a time. 'That's the . . . fucking trouble . . . with you . . . Sharon. Always fucking . . . doing things . . . for me.'

'And you're never fucking grateful.'

It sounded like a script they'd played too often in the past and I didn't want to watch a re-run. I moved away and left them to it. After a few more exchanges they were both crying and Billie's breath was coming in ever shorter gasps. At this rate, I wouldn't have the forty-eight hours to work with. Eventually there was silence in the room and I could hear the birds outside and the resounding thunk of Tommy's slasher.

Billie sucked in a painful gulp of air. 'Please, please . . . please . . . no cops.' She picked up the pills and popped them into her mouth with a big gulp of brandy.

Sharon jumped forward to try to stop her but Billie swallowed and lay back with a smile on her face. 'Don't worry, sis. I've built up a lot of tolerance. Just let me dream for a bit. And, Sharon . . . ?'

'Yes.'

'I want that twenty grand.'

Sharon looked at me helplessly. 'I should just piss off and leave you and her to work it out. Taking care of Sarah, that's my responsibility.'

'Won't work, Sharon. Clement and Greaves both know you're involved. But you should get on to Sarah and tell her to stick close to her boyfriend and be careful about where they go.'

'Great. They'll love that, like being in a movie. I don't think.'

'Can't be helped. Is there any chance Clement or Greaves can find out where Sammy is?'

Sharon considered. 'No, but I take your point. Another reason why I can't just walk away. Come on, Cliff, you're the man of action who's dealt with these sorts of bastards for years. What can we do? Don't forget I'm paying you.'

I grinned. 'Out of Billie's twenty thou.'

Sharon looked at her sister on the bed. She appeared to be sleeping, but with Billie, who could be sure?

'Fuck Billie. I almost wish that sadistic prick had—'

'No you don't. I've been thinking it over. The only thing to do is to set Clement and Greaves at odds. Hope they cancel each other out.'

'How d'we do that?'

'Go easy. I haven't got that far yet.'

'You probably broke that bandy one's jaw and wrecked his dental work.'

I shrugged. 'Staying out of his way is one of the things I'm doing here.'

'It was sort of exciting though.'

'Don't get hooked on it.'

'What do you mean?'

'I've seen it happen. I've seen people, perfectly normal ones, drawn into this kind of thing and they get a taste for it. I knew a bloke like that who robbed a bank just to keep the adrenalin running after he got into some trouble that wasn't his fault.'

'Don't worry. I'm a country girl now and that's what I'm getting back to, ASA bloody P.'

21

'Cliff,' Sharon called. 'Someone's coming.'

A car had pulled up in the street. I raced into the bedroom and picked up the .38. I couldn't see how either Clement or Greaves could know where we were, but strange things happen. I stood by a window and watched the gate. Steve Kooti and Mary Latekefu came into view and hailed Tommy, still hacking away in a corner of the yard. Nothing to be done. They saw the Falcon. They went across and talked to him. Tommy gestured in the direction of the house. Perfectly natural for him to tell his nurse aunt there was a sick woman inside.

I met her at the back door. She scowled when she saw the gun in my hand, pushed me aside and went in to where Billie was sleeping—maybe.

'What in the world is going on here, Mr Hardy?' she said. 'That woman should be in hospital, and what are you doing with a gun where my nephew's working? I warn you, if you get him in any trouble I'll . . .'

Kooti appeared beside her. I'd put the gun away but he heard what she'd said and wasn't happy.

'Answer her,' he said.

Sharon came into the room. Mary Latekefu hadn't met her, saw the resemblance, but wasn't mollified. 'Your sister is very sick.'

'We had a doctor here this morning. A nurse is coming to give her some antibiotics.'

The big Polynesian woman, looking even bigger in her civvies than she had in her nurses' uniform, gave a short laugh and stalked to the back door. 'Nurse! This place is filthy. She needs proper care in a proper hospital.'

'It's a long story, Sister,' I said. 'We had to find somewhere safe for a while. I'm sure Tommy's not in any danger and he's not involved in the . . . mess.'

'What kind of mess?' Kooti asked.

'Important people, big money and some casualties.'

'What kind of casualties?'

'Fatal.'

'That's enough. We're taking Thomas out of here now and I'm reporting you to the police.'

'No!'

Tommy fronted up with his slasher over his shoulder. He had a strip of cloth tied around his forehead and his body was running with sweat. His jaw was set and his eyes were bright. He looked something like a guerrilla jungle fighter, ready to die for his cause.

'Thomas, you have to get away from these people.'

Tommy carefully leaned the slasher against the house, took off his bandanna and wiped his face. 'No, Aunty. You're wrong. Cliff here's my friend and I trust him. I'm not in any kind of trouble. I've got a job to do and I'm going to do it.'

'That woman could die and you'd—'

'A doctor came. He said she had some sort of infection

and he's treating her. If she's not improved by tonight she's going to hospital. Right, Cliff, Sharon?'

'Right,' I said, although he'd just cut my time to manoeuvre in half.

Kooti looked at his nephew with amazement. 'That's about the most I've ever heard you say at one time, Tommy.'

'Uncle Steve,' Tommy said, 'the man who owns this house trusts me, Cliff trusts me. No one much ever trusted me before. You remember what a piss-head, cone-head, fuckwit I was out at Liston? Well, I haven't had a drink or any dope for days and I don't want it.'

Mary Latekefu shook her head disapprovingly at the language, but I could see she was impressed with Tommy's resolution. Still, she was hard to move. 'Who's the doctor?'

'An old friend of mine. He's gone out on a limb for us.'

'People do that a lot for you, do they, Mr Hardy?'

'Sometimes. Billie benefited from the time she spent in the hospital, thanks to you. She doesn't seem to be having any withdrawal problems. She's been eating and drinking a bit. Apparently her temperature and other signs aren't too bad. All I can tell you is that she's in serious danger if she goes into hospital before we can . . . resolve her problem. I can't say more than that.'

'You're a smooth talker, Hardy,' Kooti said.

To my surprise, Sharon flared up. 'He's a lot more than that. Please, we just need a little more time.'

'Mary?' Kooti said.

She went back into Billie's room and was away for a few minutes while the rest of us just stood about. When she returned she looked at her watch. 'Either I get a call from this doctor by midday tomorrow reporting on her condition or what hospital she's in or I report all this to the authorities. Stephen and I are staying in Sydney for a few days. Stephen has my mobile number.'

She gave Tommy a kiss on the cheek and went down the path to the gate. Kooti shrugged as he watched Tommy pick up his tool and go back to work.

'Looks like she's running the show.'

'Yeah,' I said. 'Give us her number. I've still got yours.'

Kooti took a pen from his jacket pocket and scribbled a number on the back of a credit card receipt. 'I like the way the kid's shaping up.'

I took the slip. 'I just might need your help, Steve.'

'Call me,' he said.

Ian Sangster's nurse arrived, a no-nonsense middle-aged woman who was evidently used to Ian's individualistic style of medicine. She examined Billie, who was sleepy but responsive, put a catheter in her arm, gave her a shot and left a vial of the medication and some pills with Sharon.

'She's not too bad,' the nurse said. 'Give her those later today and the injection tomorrow morning. Here's how you do it.'

She gave Sharon clear instructions and left. The number of people who knew about our bolt-hole was mounting, but it still felt safe. It was late morning and Sharon went off to get us some lunch. Tommy finally knocked off and drank about half a litre of water. He gestured over his shoulder at the house.

'How is she?'

'Not bad. I'm hoping to have everything settled by around this time tomorrow.'

'Yeah? How?'

'I'm still working on it.'

Sharon came back with a swag of flat bread, Greek salad and dips, fruit and orange juice. We sat around a table on the back porch in the shade. Tommy hoed in, but neither Sharon nor I had much appetite. Tommy went to his room for a nap as Sharon tidied away the food.

'Hey, don't put it away. I'm as hungry as a horse.'

Billie stepped onto the porch, grabbing the doorjamb for support. The stained nightdress barely reached her knees and it had slipped off her shoulder, leaving one breast nearly bare.

'Billie, you shouldn't be up,' Sharon said.

'Fuck that. I'm feeling better. That juice the old cow put into me hit the spot.'

She took a few hesitant steps and slumped down into the chair Tommy had vacated. She tore off a few pieces of bread and used them to ferry some salad to her mouth in the approved fashion, Another couple of chunks went into the humous and eggplant dip and she chewed with enthusiasm. There was more colour in her face than I'd seen so far and her hands were steady.

'Stop looking at me like that, you,' she snapped. 'I'm okay.'

'You've had pneumonia,' I said. 'If you're not careful you could get very sick.'

The clinical word seemed to pull her up for a moment, but she waved it away and reached for the orange juice. 'Anything to give this a boost? Where's that brandy from last night?'

'We drank it,' Sharon said.

'Fuck you. Hey, lighten up, you guys. I'm going to be fine. I'm a fast healer, right, sis? Remember when I had that . . . well, never mind.'

'Clap,' Sharon said. 'At the clinic they said they'd never seen anyone get clear of it so fast.'

'That's me. Now let's talk about what's going to happen next. Where's the cute kid, by the way?'

I said, 'He's having a rest. Been working since first light. What's going to happen is that we're trying to keep you clear of Jonas Clement and Barclay Greaves, who both want you talking, then dead.'

Billie swigged orange juice from the container and didn't turn a hair. 'Clement I know, sort of; don't know the other one, but I've dealt with pricks like them before.'

Sharon snatched the drink bottle away. 'Didn't you hear what was said last night? That guy was going to torture you.'

Billie shrugged. 'Didn't happen. I don't worry about shit that doesn't happen.'

'You're impossible.'

Billie lifted a shoulder and the top of the nightdress slid further, exposing a firm breast with a large brown nipple. 'No, I'm very possible. What's Mr Resourceful here going to do next?'

Sharon slammed her fist on the table and walked away.

'Hey, bring back the fucking juice.'

When Sharon didn't respond, Billie turned her attention to me. She cupped her hand around the bare breast and teased the nipple with her fingers. 'Well?'

'Very nice,' I said. 'I bet when you were stripping you could swing the two tassels either way together, or one to the left and the other to the right.'

She laughed. 'You bet I could, while doing the fuckin' splits.'

'Bit past it now though, aren't you?'

Her eyes were dark recesses surrounded by lines, and the skin on her hands was slightly wrinkled, puckered around her wrists. For all her emaciation there was an underlying flabbiness about her, the result of years of abuse, and she seemed to be aware of it all at once. The animation left her face and she sagged in the chair. She hitched up the nightdress.

'You're an arsehole.'

'An arsehole who might stop you getting killed.'

'Yeah, well, I'm all for that as long as I get a go at the thirty grand.'

'Twenty.'

She grinned and tried to recover some of the bravado, but her bedraggled appearance and sour breath let her down. 'We might try to up the ante.'

'Don't even think it. They're out of your league.'

'How about yours?'

'We'll see. Go back to bed, Billie. You're tired.'

She went and passed Sharon on the way. They didn't speak.

Sharon picked at the crumbs on the table. 'She drives me mad, always did. Why d'you think she was so desperate about not seeing the police? I mean, with a lawyer and everything they couldn't do too much to her. She doesn't seem to be having withdrawal problems.'

'I don't know, but I agree she was desperate about it. As for the withdrawal, she's still got a fever and she's still got alcohol and Valium in her system. It might hit her yet.'

'God help everyone if it does. Now, I heard what you said to Tommy and his uncle about getting things sorted out. Sounds as if you've got a plan.'

'It's sketchy.'

'Are you going to tell me what it is?'

'Better you don't know. For your own good.'

She stared out at the work-in-progress yard and made an exasperated grunt. 'Men are always telling women what's for their own good, instead of letting them decide for themselves.'

'I suppose that's true. In this case . . .'

'When's it going to change?'

I got up, reaching for my notebook which is never far from hand. 'When you rule the world,' I said.

'Roll on the day.'

She wandered out into the back yard, picked up a rake and started to tidy up some of Tommy's rougher spots. I checked the numbers and dialled the radio station owned and performed on by Jonas Clement.

'2BC FM.'

'I have an important message for Mr Jonas Clement.'

'I'll put you through to his secretary.'

When the secretary came on the line I asked to speak to Clement and was told he wasn't available.

'I understand that,' I said. 'I have a very important message for him. You should get this down word for word, okay? Tell him that Cliff Hardy called—he knows the name—and that if he wants to learn something about his son he should meet me tomorrow at eleven fifty am at the coffee shop on the top level of the Queen Victoria Building, Town Hall end. He's to come alone and be strictly prompt. Have you got that?'

'I think so. But what—?'

'Just read it back.'

She did and had it pretty right. I corrected a few things. She didn't like it and tried to press for more personal details but I overrode her. 'Just get that message to Clement or I guarantee you won't have a job tomorrow.'

I cut the connection, rang Oceania Securities and went through the same procedure, except that the message to Barclay Greaves referred to Clive McGuinness rather than Clement's son and the time I specified was midday.

I put the phone down and nodded to Tommy as he went past me out into the yard. He and Sharon wrestled for the rake and both laughed when Tommy let Sharon win. It was the most light-hearted moment I'd seen in some time and it gave me a lift. Then I put in a call to Hank Bachelor. I'd told Clement and Greaves to come alone, but I didn't believe they would and neither would I.

Why is it that, with emails and mobile phones, people are harder to get in touch with than ever? Probably because they move around more. There's spam, so they put off reading emails or wipe them by mistake; the mobiles go on the blink, run out of charge and there are blank spots where they don't work. Whatever the reason, I couldn't get in touch with Hank. I was swearing about it when Lily Truscott rang me.

She doesn't beat around the bush, Lil. 'Anything on Greaves yet?'

'Not yet. Maybe soon.'

'Like when?'

'Don't hold the page, Lil. Put in an ad.'

'I'm not the editor anymore, remember? Oh well, is there anything I can do for you?'

'Thanks. No. Why?'

'You sound stressed, Cliff. Not your upbeat self.'

We talked for a while about nothing in particular and I felt better. I changed into my gym gear and helped

Tommy in the yard so that by evening I was tired. Tommy, Sharon and I cleaned up the remainder of the lunch food as well as plenty of toast. Billie slept or sulked. I slept.

22

I'd been in the QVB a few weeks before buying audio books for my daughter Megan at the ABC shop on the second level of the three-gallery structure. She was going on tour with a theatre company—a lot of boring bus travel. Megan's an addicted reader but, like me, she gets sick trying to read in a bus. Okay on trains and planes. I got her *The Woman in White* and *The Surgeon of Crowthorne.* Seemed like a balanced selection. I remembered noticing that the coffee shop had been busy, and I wanted plenty of people around when I confronted Clement and Greaves, to deter them, or more likely their backups, from doing anything violent.

After her additional doses of antibiotics, Billie was feeling a lot better in the morning and was beginning to harass Sharon about her money. I told Sharon to hold off until the afternoon when I hoped to be able to report some development. I had no real expectations; I just wanted to break the deadlock and see where the chips fell.

Clement and Greaves had to be in the dark about a number of things. Clement didn't know that Rhys Thomas was really working for Greaves. God knows what he'd been told about the death of his son. It depended on how Thomas and Kezza had played it, but it was unlikely to be the truth. Greaves had to be wondering about McGuinness and what had happened to the woman he'd had abducted and paid out money for with no result.

With the two women squabbling and Tommy sweating as the day promised to be a scorcher, I was happy to leave Lilyfield. After sleeping in my underwear and sporting a three-day-old shirt, I wasn't feeling fresh. For my own sake, I wanted something to happen, almost anything.

Before leaving the house I wiped Jonas Clement's gun clean of my prints and put it in a green bag. It was a Beretta nine millimetre with the latest word in silencers attached. Highly illegal, but a nice gun if you like guns.

Thomas's pistol was a Glock. There was blood on it—Thomas's or Clement's, I couldn't be sure which. But I'd only handled it by the muzzle so that Thomas's prints were still on the butt. I wiped the muzzle carefully and put it in with the other one. I wrapped a plastic bag around the handles of the green bag. When I took it off there'd be no prints of mine.

Hank Bachelor hadn't been available so I called Steve Kooti. I had the feeling that Kooti, despite his sincerity in turning over a new leaf, still hankered deep down for something more exciting.

'I just want you there as a presence,' I said. 'You don't have to say or do anything.'

'What if I want to say or do something?'

'I'll trust your judgement.'

'And this gets the mess cleared? Tommy can get on with his job and that?'

'I hope so.'

'You don't fill me with confidence, Hardy.'

'Mate, I play it by ear. Are you in?'

'I'm in.'

I found a parking place near the old Fairfax building in Jones Street and walked the rest of the way. The promised thirty-eight degrees were rapidly approaching and I was sweating by the time I got to the QVB. As arranged, I met Kooti on the escalator and we went up to the top level. Then he hung back and I went along to where a row of tables sits beside the gallery. It was eleven fifty exactly and Clement was there. He looked a very different man from the one I'd seen at his party not long back. His face was pale and drawn; his tie knot was slipped down and his shirt was crumpled. He fiddled nervously with the sugar sachets on the table.

I circled stealthily and came up behind him. 'Don't turn round,' I said. 'I'm Hardy and this is your boy's gun.'

I dropped the green bag at his feet.

'Rhys Thomas was quicker on the draw. His gun's in here, too, with his prints on it.'

He half turned, then stopped the movement. Out of the corner of my eye I saw Thomas standing almost hidden by a pillar twenty metres away.

'What the hell do you mean?'

'I don't know what he told you, but Thomas shot your son. I was there. I saw it. He's working for Barclay Greaves. Speak of the devil, here he is.'

Greaves came striding towards us; he was early and agitated. Clement gave a roar of anger. He sprang from his seat and rushed at Greaves, who saw me, stopped and looked confused. Clement swung a wild punch that caught Greaves on the side of the head. He threw up his hands, lost his balance and hit the rail. His arms flailed and it seemed he might right himself, but he was clawing at thin air and he went over. His head cracked on the rail a level below. He let out a strangled cry and fell the rest of the way to the ground. Had to be thirty metres.

They say people sometimes witness violent scenes in the streets, think it's a movie shoot, and move on. Not this time. Women screamed, men yelled, children rushed to the rail and were hauled back. Clement stood still, rooted to the spot by shock. I spoke quickly into his ear. 'Tell the police where Scriven is and they'll go easy on you.'

I drifted away, signalling for Kooti to do the same as the crowd hemmed Clement in. I heard someone say his name and then mobile phones were out and the circus was in town.

As I moved away I noticed Thomas disappear down the stairs. If Greaves had had a minder I didn't see him. Kooti and I took the escalator down. The police and ambulance sirens were sounding before we reached the bottom. The area was empty, everyone either clearing out or gravitating to where Greaves had fallen.

Like all bouncers and enforcers, Steve Kooti had seen some rough things in his time—eyes gouged out and ears bitten off—so he wasn't too fazed, but he shook his head several times and didn't speak until we were out in the street. 'You set that up.'

'I swear I didn't. I thought they'd talk money.'

'What was that you gave him?'

'His son's pistol, complete with silencer.'

'So he's standing there with a hundred witnesses. He's bloody killed someone, and he's holding an illegal weapon. The man's in deep trouble.'

'Save your sympathy, Steve. Have you ever heard him

on the radio? Heard his views on minorities, welfare, single mothers?'

'Yeah, he's no loss. And the other one's dead. I'll pray for them. You've made a clean sweep, Hardy.'

'I'm not patting myself on the back. If the cops get on to the security camera tapes I'm in for a rough trot.'

'Okay, that's your problem. But does this clear the decks? I mean . . .'

'Tommy'll be on his own in Lilyfield in an hour and none of this'll touch him.'

We reached Goulburn Street; he hesitated and then put out his hand, swallowing mine in his big, hard grip. We shook and he walked away, head and shoulders taller than the mostly Asian people around us.

I stopped at a pub in George Street, bought a double scotch, and took it to a stool where I could sit and look out through a tinted window at Sydney on the move. Tinted windows soften the reality and I needed some softening just then. I'd been so focused on setting up the meeting, hoping for some sort of outcome, that Greaves's fall hadn't touched me emotionally. It did now. Like a lot of people, I've had falling nightmares. That terrifying feeling of being launched into space with no prospect of rescue and enough time to anticipate the contact resulting in oblivion or, worse, paralysis. Greaves had taken the fall for real, in real time, and the nightmare for him was a reality.

I sipped the drink and told myself he'd probably caused the death of Lou Kramer and would most likely have disposed of Billie Marchant once she'd told him what he wanted to know. McGuinness, his undercover man, was a sleaze and Greaves's plan to blackmail Peter Scriven was in no way in the public interest. No loss.

After the first drink and those thoughts, I felt a little better and bought another because something else was still niggling. I worked at it but couldn't tease it out. Needing food for fuel or comfort, I invested in a steak sandwich, with fries. When had they stopped being chips? I was a bit drunk as I ate the food without tasting it. The security camera was a worry, but would they have them focused on the coffee area and the ABC shop rather than the jewellery shops on all levels? Maybe not.

I tramped back through the steamy heat to the car. It had picked up a ticket. Poetic justice. I sat in it for a while with the window down, hoping for a breeze. In Jones Street, in Ultimo? No chance. I decided I was sober enough to drive and started the motor. As always, the case was still buzzing in my head and, not unusually, there were unresolved questions. Principally, what did Billie know and would I ever find out?

I steered overcautiously through the back streets until I realised that I was heading towards Glebe and home, instead of Lilyfield. Not as sober as I thought. I stopped, took a series of deep breaths, and then the disturbing subliminal thought came through to me: I remembered thinking, when I was in the QVB, wandering around after buying the talking books for Megan, how low the railing seemed and what a long drop it was to the bottom.

23

There was an air of gloom at Lilyfield. Tommy was chopping away but without his usual enthusiasm. Sharon was sitting on the back steps with a sketch pad and a pencil but looking as if her heart wasn't in it. I'd been hoping to tell the tale, reassure everyone that the troubles were over. No way.

'What?' I said.

Sharon made a few angry strokes. 'Billie's gone.'

I gave Tommy a thumbs-up and sat down beside Sharon. 'Tell me.'

'She was a lot better, obviously. She said she wanted to go. I said she couldn't until you got back. She threatened to go out on the street naked and flag down the first car. She'd have done it, too. So I had to do what she asked.'

'Which was?'

'I drove into Leichhardt, got five hundred bucks from the bank and bought her some clothes and other stuff. Got myself this pad for something to do. She had a shower, got dressed, took the rest of the money and split. Said she'd contact me.'

'She went on foot?'

'No, taxi—the phone's on now. So, what's been happening? Will one of those bastards track her down? Billie doesn't exactly go about things quietly.'

I told her what had happened and how Clement would have too much trouble on his hands to worry about Billie. She took it in without much joy. 'So there's a few people dead more or less over her, and we still don't know what she knew or why she was so shit scared of the cops.'

'Right, but at least it gets things straightened out. She's not in any danger except from herself and you can go back to Picton and tell Sarah she doesn't have to worry.'

She got up, tore off the sheet she'd been working on, crumpled it and dropped it on the ground. 'Yes. I'll do just that.'

Tommy looked enquiringly over as Sharon stomped into the house. She came out a few minutes later with her bag on her shoulder, jiggling her keys.

'I'll send you a cheque.'

I shook my head. 'Don't worry about it.'

She nodded and went to where Tommy had paused in his work. She kissed him on the cheek and went through the gate to her car in the street.

Tommy watched her go and came across to where I was smoothing out the drawing. 'Hey, Cliff, I thought you and her might be . . .'

'No,' I said.

The sketch was a portrait of Billie in full flight—hair flying, mouth open, fists clenched. It wasn't finished, just an outline, but it spoke volumes about the way she'd behaved.

Tommy sucked in a breath as he looked at it. 'Yeah, that's how she was. Didn't know what the fuck to do.'

'Nothing *to* do, mate. But now I'd like you to ring your aunty and explain that Billie's shot through. Tell her she was a lot better and that she was going to see her own doctor.'

'You want me to lie to Aunt Mary?'

'It wouldn't be the first time, would it? You can get round her better than me.'

He went into the house and I sat there as the afternoon sun lit up the yard and started to cast shadows from the taller trees. In time it was going to be a fine space for gardening, sitting, drinking, talking. I could imagine Mike there with his family having a great Italian time. Myself visiting.

Tommy came out, swigging from a litre bottle of diet coke. 'It's cool,' he said. 'Didja get everything sorted?'

'It kind of sorted itself. I'm pushing off now, Tommy.'

'I'm goin' to miss all this. I mean, like, doctors and nurses, good looking chick artist and a junkie and a detective. Like being on TV.'

'Are you going to be all right here?'

'How do you mean?'

'It's hard work and you're all alone. Easy to think, "Fuck it, I need some fun." You know.'

'Yeah, I know. Being a black cone-head on the dole isn't fun. I've got a chance here with Mike and I'm gonna grab it.'

'Are you going to look up your father?'

'Thinkin' about it.'

I folded the incomplete sketch and stuck it in my pocket. We shook hands.

'Thanks, Cliff,' Tommy said.

I wasn't sure that I'd earned it, but I accepted it anyway, from him.

. . .

A storm had been building all day and it broke as I was driving home. First, some big hailstones pelted down, big enough for me to feel them crunching under the wheels and to make me worry about the windscreen. The rain followed in bucketfuls; the gutters overflowed within minutes and we drivers were slowed to a crawl while trying to keep the revs up through water that was axle-high across dips in the roads.

I parked outside my house, collected my bits and pieces and got thoroughly soaked just getting to the front door. I didn't care. The air needed clearing, the dust needed laying, and I needed a shower anyway.

24

The security cameras had picked me up and the police hauled me in. Detective Senior Sergeant Piers Aronson, who I'd dealt with before, interviewed me in the Glebe detectives' room. I had my solicitor, Viv Garner, present and I wasn't expecting to have much fun. Aronson switched on the recording equipment, identified himself, me and Viv, and got down to it.

'You were present in the Queen Victoria Building when Barclay Greaves was killed?'

'Yes.'

'How did you come to be there?'

'I arranged the meeting between Jonas Clement and Greaves to try to resolve a matter I was working on.'

'That matter was . . . ?'

'Confidential between my client and myself.'

'You don't have that privilege,' Aronson said.

Viv said, 'It's a moot point, Senior. Depending on the client. I suggest you move on.'

Aronson didn't like it, but he wasn't about to make an issue of it at this stage. 'You handed a bag to Jonas Clement.'

'Did I?'

'Video evidence says you did.'

'Those videos are fuzzy and jumpy and people cross the line and make the action confusing in my experience,' Viv said. 'Are Mr Hardy's fingerprints on this alleged bag?'

Aronson wasn't going to fall into a question and answer session. 'You provoked Clement into attacking Greaves. What did you say to him?'

'I forget. What does Clement say I said?'

I'd told Viv all I needed to convince him that I hadn't meant to bring about Greaves's death. His advice was answer questions like this with a question about Clement, who would certainly be getting the best possible legal advice himself. Ride piggyback on Clement's high-price brief.

Aronson's reaction confirmed Viv's advice. He was discomfitted, almost angry. Clement had told them nothing damaging to me, possibly nothing at all. Aronson kept it up for as long as he could, hammering away at my lack of confidentiality protection, my absenting myself from the scene and my conviction some time back for destroying evidence and obstructing justice. Viv and I fended him off enough so that he eventually finished the interview.

I thanked Viv and he left. I stayed where I was because I knew Aronson and I hadn't finished.

'Off the record, Hardy, I'm going to go after your licence as strong as I can. You've been up to some shit here and I'm sure you caused that man's death. Does any of that worry you?'

'The death, no. The licence, yes.'

'Good. You can expect to hear from the appropriate people. I think you're gone.'

'I've been through it before and survived.'

'Your luck's run out.'

'We'll see. I tell you what, Piers. When you lot get a conviction against Jonas Clement and have him safely locked away for, oh, five to ten for manslaughter, we can get together and I'll tell you all about it.'

That's how we left it. I'm still waiting to hear about the suspension of my licence, which is a good sign. The system is that suspension is followed by a searching interview with all sorts of bureaucratic bullshit, before an absolute de-licensing can happen. I'm still hopeful.

I followed the Clement case in the papers. Greaves, who was described as a financial adviser, had been dead on arrival, of course. Clement was charged with murder initially but the charge was reduced to manslaughter. Legal technicalities delayed the case coming to trial and it could be a while longer before it's heard. Rumour has it that Clement's defence is going to claim that the death of his son placed him under a strain and reduced his responsibility for his actions. Clement Junior's death was attributed to an accident. Might work.

Whether Clement used his information about Peter Scriven as a bargaining chip, I don't know. In any case it was no business of mine. Scriven had chiselled honest people out of their businesses and savings and if he was being bled by Clement that was all right with me. They never recover any money from these crooks who do a runner anyway.

Tommy did a terrific job at Mike's place and went on to do the painting and repair work. Still at it, and Mike's promised him a job driving when he's finished. I drop around there from time to time and always come away thinking I should get someone to do a job on my place. Never get around to it, though.

I went to Frank and Hilde's on election night, looking forward to seeing them but not expecting any joy. They had a few other people over, ex-cops, social workers—the area Hilde had gone into—and tennis club friends. It was a good group, lively, with a good gender mix and a range of political positions that meant the results pleased some and displeased others. There was a good deal of chiacking in an Aussie way that really says we think all politicians are bastards at heart.

Interest went out of the result very early and people started to drift away. Frank took me aside around 11 pm. We were both a bit depressed by the outcome, both a bit drunk.

'I hear you're sailing close to the wind with this Clement thing, mate,' Frank said.

'Yeah, I'm looking at a licence hearing. You going character witness for me?'

'Did it before an' I'll do it again. You could be out on your ear.'

'Viv Garner reckons just a suspension.'

'Viv's a bloody optimist, always was. Cliff, have you ever thought of packing it in and doing something else?'

'Like what?'

'I dunno. You need a business plan. Sell that bloody great terrace and buy a flat and invest the balance and . . .'

'Yeah, Frank?'

'Fuck it, you won't.'

He was right there.

Lily Truscott had agreed to come to the party with me even though I hadn't been able to follow through with any dope on Greaves. Harry Tickener was there too, and he told me the publishers were trying to see if there was anything they could do with the draft bits of manuscript they'd got from Lou Kramer on Clement now that he was in the news. They were playing it very close to the chest so there was nothing for Harry. I'd disappointed them both, and we were all depressed by the election. But Lily came back to my place and stayed the night so the evening wasn't a total loss.

I got a cheque from Sharon in the mail although I hadn't submitted an account. Enclosed in the envelope was a caricature of a bloke with grizzled grey-black hair, a broken nose, suspicious eyes and a humorous expression. Can't think who it could be.

Steve Kooti stays in touch with Tommy and I've run into him once or twice. He tells me that nothing much has changed out at Liston. John Manuma's protection centre is still working its scams and the Island Brotherhood was celebrating the conservative victory in the federal election.

'That'd be right,' I said to him. 'What about your mob?'

'Greens.'

I didn't hear anything more about Rhys Thomas and for a while I watched out for bow-legged men with attitude, but I didn't really expect to run into him. If he was smart he'd be far, far away, but given Clement's connections there was a good chance that he was dead and buried.

I thought that was it, filed the contracts, my notes on the case, the photos I'd taken outside Lou's apartment block and Sharon's sketch, and got on with other things, but Sharon turned up at my office one day out of the blue. She was in her overalls and sneakers so she wasn't there to take me to lunch at the Mixing Pot. I sat her down and brewed some coffee.

She tasted it and pulled a face. 'That's terrible,' she said.

'I can't make good coffee,' I admitted. 'It's always bitter. Other people use my gear and it turns out fine, but I can't do it.'

'Have you got anyone yet, Cliff? You know—a significant other?'

'No, not really. You?'

'Might have. We'll see, but I came to tell you about Billie. She rang me and said she wanted to see me. She's in Newcastle. I thought what the hell, good place, be a change, so I drove up there.'

'When was this?'

'Two days ago. Of course, she wanted the rest of the money but that wasn't why she wanted to see me. I mean, I could've sent her a cheque. So I went to her flat—nice place in the heart of the city. She looked pretty good—tarty as hell, but that's Billie. She told me she was working in a high-class brothel. Drove me round a bit in her Celica, although she lost her licence a few years ago. Secondhand car but pretty good. She showed me the brothel, looked all right as such places go—not that I'd know.

'But she was as nervous and edgy as anything. I thought it was the speed or the smack, but she swore she was off everything except a little coke sometimes to help her through the night. She was smoking something fierce but she always did, from the age of, I dunno, ten?

'Okay, so we go back to her flat and she opens a bottle of wine. I give her a cheque for the rest of the money—after what I paid you and a few of my expenses. She hardly looks at it and then it comes out. I bet you can guess.'

'Sammy,' I said.

'Right. She wants him back. I mean, there she is, hooking in Newcastle, using coke, probably up to here in debt and she wants her kid.'

'What did you do?'

'Well, I thought about it for like, a tenth of a second. But then I thought back to all the crap we'd been through—you getting bashed and seeing two people get killed, and the threats to me and Sarah—and we still didn't know what they all wanted from her.'

I nodded. 'Pissed me off for a while, but I've got used to untidy endings.'

'I'm not. I sort of strung her along and asked her why she was so afraid of the cops. Remember that?'

'Yes.'

'She hemmed and hawed and didn't want to tell me but I had her over a barrel, so she did. She killed Eddie.'

'Jesus. Did she say how?'

'She said she got him drunk and pushed him down some steps. She said he'd found out about Sammy and was calling her a mongrel bitch with a mongrel kid. She'd had enough and did for him. Didn't mean to kill him, she said, but she reckoned crippled'd do.'

'Rings true, doesn't it? Eddie was a real piece of shit.'

'Yeah.' Sharon drank some more of the coffee, as bad as

it was. I could see that she needed to go on and that she hadn't got to the hardest part yet. I waited.

'So I let her think that had got her some points and I asked her about what Eddie had told her about that guy who'd skipped. All the stuff you told me about—where he is and that.'

'And?'

'She laughed her head off. She said she didn't know a fucking thing about it. Zip, zilch. Funniest fucking thing in the world. She let that Kramer woman think she knew something. Just big-noting herself, and hoping she might get something out of it in some way. That's what started all this off and she didn't give a stuff. She's a moral zero, Cliff, my own sister.'

There was nothing to say. I sat there and a silence seemed to fill the room, although the traffic noise from King Street must still have been coming through. But that's the way it is in some moments, when the weight of what's being said just kind of hits the mute button.

Sharon sucked in a breath. 'Know what I did? I'd prepared myself for this. I had a photo of Sammy, taken a fair while after Billie had last seen him. Since I'd found him the place where he'd be looked after. Here it is.'

She reached into her pocket and pulled out a polaroid photo. It showed an adolescent boy, clearly the same person as in the earlier photograph I'd seen. He'd grown, gained confidence, and looked ready to take the next steps.

I nodded and handed it back.

'I was cruel,' Sharon said. 'I showed her the picture. She tried to snatch it from me. Screamed, tried to scratch. I held on to it and I decked her.'

Sharon, crying now, quietly, not out of control, went on through her sobs: 'She was on her knees, pleading . . .'

'What did you say?'

The sobs stopped and she lifted her head. 'I said no.'